WHEN DARKNESS FALLS, HE DOESN'T CATCH IT

BY: ROSS PATTERSON

DEDICATION

To the woman who made me a Hot Pocket after we fucked at your studio apartment; even though you were super poor, that HP meant a lot. Mostly because I realized on my way out to my limo the next morning that I probably just took away an entire meal from you. I'm sorry I didn't call you after that, I just didn't want to. Truthfully, I wouldn't have even fucking remembered you if this commercial for Hot Pockets wouldn't have just appeared on the satellite TV inside my yacht. Be grateful that it did so you can tell your friends that you're mentioned in a fucking book.

TABLE OF CONTENTS

PROLOGUE

June 10th, 2015 1am
McSorley's Old Ale House. New York, NY

You're goddamn right I'm still sitting at the same weathered wooden table in the back of Manhattan's oldest bar where I just finished my first masterpiece *At Night She Cries, While He Rides His Steed*. The second I finished it, I started writing this one. I'm now 14 beers deep, and I've polished off an entire eight ball of yay. The phrase "everything in moderation" applies to everything except cocaine, booze, and prostitutes. If you haven't read my last book then you probably won't understand anything in this book, so you should probably go buy that first and stop being poor. It's fucking gross.

Let's get something straight, my life is so important that you should be grateful I'm even doing this. Seriously, do you know another motherfucker like me? Me neither. So let's get down to brass, in the last book I told you that I was going to off myself after completing my life story. That still holds true. My trusty handgun is still loaded next to my Remington Rand typewriter that Hemingway pissed on, and you know the fucking bartender isn't going to cut me off, so I'm going to sit here and keep writing my memoirs until I finish. To answer your question, no, I haven't gotten up for bathroom breaks. I just piss on the floor. That's what we used to do in the old days, and since this is the oldest bar in New York City, they still let you do it—but only if you are still alive from that era, and I am the only one left. Don't forget, I'm still 186 years old.

Once my memoirs are completed, that's when I blow my fucking brains out. I'm not going to use an exercise band and a Carabiner like a fucking pussy. I'm squeezing the trigger and going out like a fucking man. I've got enough coke on me to last several days, so it could be a few more books. I will tell you this though, after living 186 years on this earth, I know the exact date when it all went to shit. When men stopped being men. When the world lost it's urge to reach down and grab its dick and balls, then wipe that hand across someone's beak. On that date in my life, that's where I'll end it. If you're a real *hombre*, you know deep down when that date was. If not, take another nibble out of your "milligram controlled" weed edible and keep reading to hopefully become a man someday. Fuckface.

~Whatever the opposite of "sincerely" is ~ St. James St. James

Chapter 1

A NEW CHAPTER FOR ME...
BOTH LITERALLY AND FIGURATIVELY

April 30th, 1862
Philadelphia, Pennsylvania

For the last three years, I've spent my life on the run in what would turn out to be the most notorious manhunt in United States history. Motherfuckers from all walks of life have to tried to take a shot at the title, and I've killed all of them in spectacular fashion. Every law dog and country bumpdick who wanted to make a name for himself by trying to claim the massive bounty on me ended up with a bullet in his head, and one in each nut. I wasn't Lance Armstrong-ing dudes, I was taking out both—with one exception—but we'll get to him later.

I'm also proud to say that I was the first man ever to have an all nude *Wanted Poster*. It was a full body drawing in "Landscape" mode, which was innovative at the time. Andy Warhol would later go on to recreate it as a painting so he could masturbate to it. After briefly losing his sight, he eventually sold it and gave all the proceeds to a charity for underprivileged albino children. Sunblock must be expensive. I wouldn't know, I've never touched that shit because I'm not a fucking gimp. I tan hard.

These days, I've traveled as far east across this beautiful country as my steed can take me, but I still haven't found Samantha Davis. He's one of the only friends I've had who works for slave wages, and I've missed him for that reason. Real barbershop talk, it's fucking lonely out here, and the strain of losing my family three years ago has worn on me. I haven't been with a woman since my wife Louretta died. Sorry, that's not true. I think I just wanted to write it down on paper to hear how it sounded... *and it sounds fucking ridiculous.*

I've actually put my dick inside everyone I could, even though I look dirtier than the *Trivago* guy. When you're this famous, women just throw pussy at you. It's pretty fucking insane. The fame thing has never really changed over the course of my 186 years on this earth. Everybody wants to bang, and obviously I deliver the goods in the sack, so that legend keeps growing. I'd be lying to you if I said I hadn't found myself longing for the home life I once had, obviously during the "rich times". Being poor again is a real motherfucker. I can't stress how much of a damper it puts on your whole life sitch.

As I wander out into the forest, I don't even know where I'm going anymore. I don't own the clothes I'm wearing, and some old bed, I'll soon be sharing. I've got one more silver dollar, so I knock on the door of the first log cabin that I see with a lantern on inside of it. Maybe I can pay someone for a place to lay my dong for the evening. A small peephole in the door opens and I see a pair of surprised white eyes.

"What the hell do you want?" A woman asks.

"I need a place to stay and water for my steed. Also, a bath for myself would be nice. Philadelphia is fucking hot in the summer, who knew?"

Her eyes stare at me suspiciously for a moment, before she finally says, "Are you on the run or something?"

"Yeah. A group of Marshals burned down my house and murdered my entire family a few years back, so I killed them. Now, I'm wanted for like a hundred murders, maybe more. But that's like a whole other story about me being awesome and shit."

Her eyes grow wide and she slams the peephole shut. As I turn to walk off, she immediately bursts into laughter as she unlocks the door.

"*Shiiiiiiiiiit,* that's all you had to say! Fuck them copper badges! Come on in!" she says with open arms.

When she opens the door, I am taken back by her appearance. She's pretty, but I've never seen a woman like this before. I move in closer and gently touch her face. Her skin is as soft as velvet, but different than anything I've ever seen.

"Were you burned in a fire?" I ask.

"No. What do you mean?"

"Your skin, it's like it's been charred black," I say curiously.

"That's because *I am black.*"

"I'm sorry, I'm not following," I say to her confused.

"I was a slave. My family is from Africa," she says growing more frustrated.

"Is that a band?" I ask, still not following.

"No dipshit, *I'm a Negro.*"

"Oh, I used to sing your spirituals!"

"Say what?" She shakes her head incredulously and starts to close the door in my face.

"Wait, I'm sorry. I was born and raised out west my whole life. This is the first time I've been east of the Colorado Rockies, and you're the first black person I've ever seen."

She looks at me and laughs. "Oh yeah, there aren't any black people west of Colorado. It's too cold for that bullshit! Come on in and let's get you cleaned up. I'll explain to you what the fuck has been going down."

For the next two hours she regaled me with stories about slavery and the Civil War that is currently taking place. How could I not know what was going on in my own country? Hiding out in the woods is a real motherfucker. Yes, my beard was amazing, but socially I knew nothing. My mind was fucking blown.

Everything she told me sounded like the hell I was going through, except I was white of course. When she launched into the story of her escape from the south, we instantly bonded. It was a really special moment amongst two outlaws who gave zero fucks about authority.

The rest of the afternoon we laughed and sang some of the old Negro Spirituals that my father taught me as a boy. The song *You Better Never Run*, suddenly had new meaning to me now. I'm probably going to take it out of my repertoire for awhile, or just save it for all white dinner parties. You get it. They love that shit behind closed doors.

With the sun setting through the window, the rays beamed off her skin giving her an angelic silhouette. I could feel her getting lost in my eyes like a blind girl inside a bouncy castle, just

7

as so many other women had before her. Most of them were never found again. My eyes should come with a lifeguard on duty, because when you fall, you fucking drown. Embarrassed, she drops her washcloth. I looked down in the tub and smile knowing what was coming next. A few seconds later, the washcloth rose out of the water like the Loch Ness Monster, and I wasn't using my hands. Her face lit up in excitement.

"Here's your washcloth back," I say pointing to my dick.

"I've never met a white boy like you before," she says fanning her face.

"If we were playing poker, I'd be called a one-of-a-kind."

"That's not—that's just having one singular card," she says confused.

I stand up out of the bath, fully nude in all my glory. "Unlike a singular card, I'm not wearing a suit."

She almost faints from the sexual tension, or the fact that we're in a log cabin in the middle of July during the 1800's with no AC. Who knows, and who the fuck cares. Just because AC hadn't been invented yet, that certainly wasn't going to get in the way of my first experience with a black woman. Shit is about to be turnt the fuck up.

She leans into me and kisses me nervously, while slowly removing her dress. When it hits the ground I notice a shadow cast of her ass on the wall. It was fucking huge. A steep curve like that usually requires a road sign. I gently spin her around to get a better view, and that's when I notice large scars across her back.

"Whoa. What happened, were you mauled by live pumas as a child?" I ask.

"No. I was whipped by my white slave masters when they caught me trying to escape."

Briefly looking away, I shake my head with disgust. On the floor, I notice my belt dangling from the loops of my jeans. Upon closer examination, I see Ron's blood permanently stained into the leather from when I'd beaten him with it before. My mind suddenly fills with flashbacks of his face screaming over and over again as I whipped the shit out of him. All I could imagine was this beautiful lady being inflicted with the same pain. In that moment, I knew what I needed to do.

As this voluptuous black woman stared at me with kind eyes, I reach down and pull my belt from out of the loopholes and wrap it around her hand tightly. She looks down at the leather belt in her hand with bewilderment, as I walk over to the wall and throw my hands against it. I take a deep breath and stare at her intently.

"Tonight, you can be my slave master," I say.

"What? I—I—I can't," she gasps.

"Yes, you can. Whip me as hard as you want. I want to know what your people have been going through."

"But sir—

"Please, call me Mr. Street James."

"Mr. Street James I don't think I can—

"I've beaten many white men with my belt. I can tell you with absolute certainty there is no better feeling in the entire world. Let the belt dangle about an inch from the floor, then rise up and whip the shit out of me."

She slowly nods her head and walks behind me. The last bit of sunlight gleams off my belt buckle as the loose leather now hangs just above the floor. She squeezes her fingers and grips the buckle firmly and whips me hard across my back. My eyes lose focus for a few seconds from the pain.

"Harder," I muster.

"No, I can't—

"Beat me like I stole all your fucking soup!" I say, raising my voice to emphasize how much I want this.

She finally gives in and comes down on me with the belt harder than *Passion Of The Christ*. Holy fucking shit this hurts. I don't care how sexually advanced you are; you've never been whipped during sex harder than a former black slave whipping a white man. That *50 Shades Of Grey* bullshit was like an eight year-old Asian tapping his Xbox controller compared to this shit.

After regaining consciousness, the next few hours were like something I've never experienced before. I was bleeding, humiliated, I wondered if triceratops had a real possibility of coming back—but at the same time taken care of in a motherly way. Grabbing her huge ass, I climaxed harder than I ever have in my whole life, because I climaxed for freedom. This was the first time in the last three years that I truly felt at home. Afterward, we laid on the bed together as she fed me cornbread and applied aloe to my back.

"What are you going to do? You know the Marshals will be after you?" She whispers sweetly.

"I know they want my big dumb dick off the streets, but I am uncertain of a place to go where I don't have to look over my shoulder every five minutes. Do you know anywhere I can go and be able to kill Marshals if I need to?"

"Yeah, the Confederate soldiers are killing lawmen, and they getting away with it too. Everybody doing it down south," she says as she begins to braid my long hair.

"Fuck yeah, let's do that. Come with me," I say as my eyes light up.

"I can't. They're fighting to *keep* slavery going. You see, the south don't want us to be free, but that's the only way *you* can be free," she says sadly.

"What do you mean?" I ask.

"They giving out pardons to every soldier who fights after the war ends. Clean slate. There's your freedom," she says.

"No. Then I'll stay here with you and just keep killing people. That will be our life, you will clean up the bodies afterward. I'll chop off the head and limbs, then burn them. That's what true love is."

She smiles and squeezes my hand, genuinely considering it. Our tender moment is broken up by the sounds of hound dogs and Marshals screaming in the distance. When I run over to the window to look outside, I accidentally break through it, because I still have an erection resembling an arched crossbow.

I look down at the shards of glass and shake my head in disappointment. "Sorry, that happens all the time. By the way, there are about thirty Marshals out there who may, or may not have seen me break your window with my penis."

Her eyes grow wide with fear. "Marshals? We gotta get dressed and get the hell up out of here."

"Where are we going?" I ask.

"I know a safe house down south that will take you in. It's run by a real nice white man who helps sneak slaves up north. He'll take care of you and get you where you need to be," she says as she scoops up her clothes.

"I won't have to do any guy on guy shit in return for his help, will I? I've never been cool with that in the past."

"Maybe a little," she says with a hearty chuckle.

I run toward her and kiss her passionately, like any respectable man would do after an interracial one-night stand that fucking awesome. We dress as quickly as we can, and as I put my belt back through the loops, I notice my own blood stains on the leather. It's a nice full circle moment. Even though thirty men are trying to kill me, it's still important to appreciate the little things. Having sex with a black woman while being whipped with a belt were two huge sexual milestones for me, and I wanted to let that butter simmer for a sec.

Once I'm fully dressed, she grabs my hand and runs me out the back door. We hop on my steed, heading out into the darkness. As we rode through the woods, the echoing of barking dogs lessened and lessened, until we couldn't hear it anymore. Not fearing any imminent danger, I ease up on the reigns and slowed the pace. She shakes her head at me and digs her heels into my steed's ribs, insisting that we keep moving.

"I don't understand why you want to speed up, they're not following us anymore?" I ask her.

"If we don't get to my safe house before dawn, they'll kill me for being a runaway slave in the south. Nightfall is my only disguise. I need to drop you off and hightail it back."

She pulls a small bottle of whiskey out of her boot, pops the cork and hands it to me. I drink the entire thing and throw it out amongst the trees, knowing she probably wanted me to have the whole thing. She put her arms around me and holds me tightly as we ride through the night. I can feel my own blood soaking through the back of my shirt from the whipping I took earlier. I've never felt more alive.

Just before dawn we passed a large sign that reads, *"Virginia Welcomes You... If You're __White__."* About an hour later, we arrive at another log cabin way out in the middle of the woods. She instructs me to stay by the horse while she walks up to the door.

When I hop down and stretch out my frame, I could physically smell my crotch through my jeans. The humidity in the South was something I was going to have to get used to. My whole genital region was a small swamp jammed into an oven mitt. The smell is so pungent that I actually feel bad for my steed, because now that smell was living on him.

I pat him on his back as if to say that I was sorry, but he turns his nose the other direction, obviously pissed off. That part of being a horse sucks, you know? Just think about how many taint smells are engrained into horses after soaking through a leather saddle. It's fucking disgusting. Go take a whiff of your grandfather's bicycle seat after an easy fifteen mile ride in June. That'll give you the gist.

Peeking out from behind him, I see my lady stop at the door and knock three times, then perfectly execute a night owl call with her hands. A peephole slides open, exactly the same as her own door did. Motherfuckers didn't trust each other for shit back then. I could visibly make out the eyes and nose of a white man, but I can't hear their conversation. When they were finished talking, he slid the peephole shut and she jogs back over to me.

"He says you can stay and he'll get you where you need to go," she says, slightly out of breath.

"Thank you. What did you tell him?"

"That you were a white man who needed help. That's it. I didn't give him your name in case he knew who you were and wanted to collect a bounty. He wants you to come around through the back door though," she instructs.

"Okay," I say as she takes my hand and we walk back around the house together. "How are you going to get home? Do you want to take my steed?"

"No. I keep a horse in the stable out back. I come down here a couple times a month," she says as she points behind the house.

"Good. I wasn't going to give him to you anyway," I say with a fake laugh trying to throw her off the fact that I wasn't kidding. Knowing this is probably the final time I'll see her, I stop and pull her into me.

She smiles. "You know I don't have time for all that right now," she says.

"I know. This is the first time in my entire life that I don't know what to say," I whisper, staring deeply at her.

15

"If you had manners, you'd say 'thank you,'" she says.

That's my line. Goddamnit, she gets me. We kiss with hard tongue, before she slowly releases my hand and walks back toward the stable. As I watch her big beautiful ass walk away, it dawns on me, I don't even know her name.

"By the way, you never told me your name?"

Turning back, she smiles brightly. "It's Harriet... Harriet Tubman."

She blows me a kiss before walking into the stable, hopping up on her horse and riding out of my life forever. Watching her ride off into the distance, I thought about the historical ramifications of this woman. After all, you never forget your first black girl. As I stood there and watch her disappear on her horse, I also wondered if I was her first white man. Twenty dollars says I was. *Nailed it.*

I put my hand on my pistol and walk over to the back door and knock three times. The door slowly unlocks and creeps open. My jaw hit the floor as I stood there in shock, staring at the man standing in front of me.

There was complete silence for an entire minute before the man finally asks, "Dad?"

"Daniel? You son of a bitch! You're alive?" I ask him, genuinely surprised.

"Yeah Dad, I'm alive. You told me to go east as far as I could," he says with a huge grin.

"You have no idea how happy I am to see you. Look at you. Why is your face all red?" I ask as I begin to touch it.

"I think the gold paint I used might have be lead-based. My face has been burning for like, three years now. Come on in. Can I get you a drink?" He asks.

"Does a rapist need a reason? Of course not. Hell yes I'll take a drink!" I laugh as I embrace him tightly, genuinely touched to see my son alive.

A couple nostrils might have flared, but time makes you forget the weak shit. You see, despite all the hubris and bravado—which also happens to be yet another nickname for my dick and balls—there really is nothing like family. Especially when you might need another human shield. After our embrace ends, I breeze past him toward the middle of his cabin.

"You got any whores or drugs in here? Also, it too early for coke? Personally, I can do it all day."

Daniel shakes his head and shuts the door looking over at me as I sit down and kick my boots up on the kitchen table. He walks over and hands me a glass of whiskey, which I immediately toss down my gullet. I slam the glass on the table and swipe the entire bottle out of his hands and begin to drink out of it.

"Dad, can you take your feet off the table? My wife is coming home any minute with dinner and she will be pissed."

"Is this a sick fucking joke? You're married at your age? You piece of shit," I say with disdain.

Daniel sighs deeply, lowering his head. "Dad, I'm twenty-two years old—

He knows what's coming next. "If you have a cat, I swear to fuck, I'll lop your balls clean off your body and stitch you a handmade vagina deep enough for eight full inches of insertion—

"Dad, I don't have a fucking cat. I just got married, that's it. No gay shit either, okay? I married a real fine piece of ass considering my whole shit going on up here," he says as he motions to his reddish face.

I take a long pull of whiskey and nod my head, acknowledging his skin condition. "You probably should have led with the psoriasis condish before the wife thing. BT Dubs, if you're holding any coke, that was more than a hint earlier."

Daniel sighs. "Good to see you, Dad."

Chapter 2

SOUTHERN COMFORT ISN'T JUST A SHITTY WHISKEY

With the whiskey now gone, I walk around his kitchen examining the place as I calmly pound a large mug of ale from a wooden jug, before slamming it on the table demanding more. As a chaser, I double penetrate a mason jar of moonshine that I found in one of the cabinets. I'm definitely tying one the fuck on tonight. I look up above the kitchen sink and see a sign that reads, "The St. James' Home: Live, Laugh, Love." That's when I lose all of my shit.

"What the fuck bro? Engraved moniker signage in the kitchen? What the shit does live, laugh, love even mean? It sounds like some bullshit you hear from women over thirty who aren't married," I bristle.

"It was Penelope's idea," he says very weakly.

"Jesus Christ, man. Does your outhouse have a sign in it that says, 'Pee. Sitting. Down?'"

The door suddenly opens and beautiful southern woman in her early twenties, Penelope, walks in with an enormous hoop skirt as she folds an umbrella. When she turns and sees me, she stops and clutches her huge heaving chest, somewhat startled. I fake tip my hat, even though I'm wearing one and probably just could have given it a tug if I wasn't so fucked up.

"Sorry Daniel, I was unaware that we were entertaining guests," she says.

"I wasn't either, my love. Penelope, this is my father, Saint James Street James," he says motioning to me.

Penelope extends her hand and curtsies. "Oh my gosh. Daniel has said so much about you. It is a pleasure, sir."

"I know. It usually is." Instead of kissing her hand, I stand up and move in for a super awkward drunk hug that smashes her hoop skirt upward, knocking a bunch of shit off the counter. I smile as I look into a mirror on the wall behind her, catching a glimpse of her ass and panties. Daniel knows exactly what I'm doing and he shakes his head.

"Okay Dad, that's enough. How about we have some dinner?"

I give a real slow release, exhaling deeply. "You still killing bald eagles Daniel?"

"Daniel did you used to kill bald eagles?" She asks in shock.

"Ummmm, nope. We just have some traditional food from town, pop."

"Well, let's do whatever the fuck that is then. If there's any vegetables, throw them out the fucking window."

Penelope gives Daniel a look of confusion as he shrugs his shoulders. I sit back down at the kitchen table and proceed to light a hand rolled cigarette that is tucked away inside my duster jacket. Letting out a small whistle, I shake my empty mug at Penelope indicating that I need a refill ASAP. For good measure, I mouth the words "fill this the fuck up". She forces a smile, grabs the mug, and walks back to the kitchen.

I don't even bother asking for an ash tray, the floor is fine and I'm sure she'll clean it sometime afterward. Looking around the house, I spot a portrait of Louretta. She's sitting on a crushed red velvet chair smiling.

"You know, I've always loved that picture of your mother. I'm surprised you have it," I say with a hint of nostalgia.

"After I was shot all those times protecting you so you could escape California, I ended up going back to our house that

21

burned down after I healed up. I found this portrait still intact underneath the ashes, so I took it with me. It's the only memory I have of her," he says with a twinge of sadness.

"That's beautiful Daniel. I remember the night I painted it actually."

"*You* painted this?"

"I sure did. Right after we boned. We had gotten into an argument after her third climax and I threw all her clothes out of the window," I say remembering back with a smile.

"Dad, I don't know if I want to hear this—

"You should hear this, Daniel. This picture has unbelievable meaning to me."

Penelope walks in and hands me a beer, then stops to listen to the rest of story. I take a huge swig and focus back in on the picture, while rubbing the rim of my beer mug. Like a baby elk in quick sand, I'm barely able to keep my head up and hold a thought.

"As I was saying, during her third or possibly fourth orgasm, she screamed out 'Oh, Ryan'. Now, I don't know that fucking dude, nor had I invited him in as a casual observer to soft swing that night, so I picked up her clothes and threw them out the fucking window. She looks at me and says, "No, *Orion*, the constellation," and she points out the window into the sky. I don't know what the fuck a constellation is, so I draw my pistols and start firing out the window blasting holes through all her clothes. After about an hour of her explaining what all the bullshit stars mean, I dunk my ding-a-ling in a cold glass of water and cool off. I decided to make it up to her by spontaneously painting her a portrait."

Daniel stares at me confused, "But she's wearing a dress in the portrait?"

"I added that later for you guys. All eight of you boys were just kids, so I painted a dress on her since it was hanging in our living room, but—

I pull a penny out of my pocket and walk toward the portrait and lean in. "If you scratch it off, you can see her whole world."

Slowly I begin to gently rub the penny against the dress and the paint chips off revealing her huge tits and gigantic bush underneath the cheap added layer of paint. Penelope gasps in horror. I take a step back to admire the large portrait, which now reveals Daniel's mother fully nude. It's been a long time since this pic has been in front of me, and to be honest, I'm a little bit emotional. I take a deep breath and absorb my masterpiece.

"Goddamnit I miss that bush. I used to get lost in it for hours," I say longingly.

"Well, I'm going to go make dinner," Penelope blurts out, probably trying to avoid this weird situation.

"Can I get a top off on this brew dog?" I ask, still admiring Louretta's bush. Daniel puts his head down in shame. I flick an ash on the floor from my heater.

"Sure. How about an ashtray too?" She asks curtly.

"I don't really give a fuck about the ashtray, I'm sure you're going to sweep up tomorrow, so it's your call on that," I say as I throw the cigarette butt on the floor and stomp it out with my boot.

"I'll get you one anyway. We call that southern hospitality down here," she says forcing a polite smile.

As she walks away I whisper to Daniel, "Guess she hates cleaning. Have fun when your kids start smoking. What is she going to tell them? To smoke *outside*? That'll never goddamn happen in this life," I say as I walk back over to the dining room and sit down.

About an hour later, there's an ashtray full of cigs on the table, and I've worked up a near blackout buzz. Daniel seems a little more relaxed too as he laughs and jokes with me like the old days. I give him a strong gooch punch as Penelope walks in with the plates of food she has prepared and puts them on the table in front of us.

I take a long hard stare at the meal. "What the fuck is this?"

"It's rice, peas, beans, dried fruit, potatoes, molasses, and salted pork with a little dash of vinegar," she says like she's made it a hundred times before.

I nod impressed. "Well, fuck my cock. That is a beautiful spread."

"Thank you, Mr. Street James. That means a lot—

"Sorry, I'm actually referring to my dead wife's bush still," I say pointing at the portrait of Louretta on the wall. "But by all means, please join us, Penelope."

"Uh, sure. I'd love to," she says as she grabs a plate of food and walks out, taking a seat next to Daniel. Penelope grabs his hand and extends her other hand to me for me to hold. I look at her slightly puzzled.

"It's time for a prayer," she says softly.

"You think I'm a Pagan?" I ask as I pick up a knife off the table. "I'll cut my fucking arm open right now to prove I'm not a witch—

"Dad, stop! We say a prayer to Jesus thanking him for the food before we eat," Daniel says in a hushed tone.

"The only prayer I've ever heard you say was right before you fucked that prostitute in my opium den when you were fourteen. I remember because I was right next to you laughing," I say.

Penelope's eyes grow wide as Daniel's face turns even redder than it naturally is now. "Dad! We just say a simple prayer in thanks for the meal. It's tradition down here. That's it. I'll lead us—

"No, if we're saying a prayer, why don't you hop in the back of the dinghy and let me take the oars on this one."

"That's not necessary DAD—

I clear my throat three times as loud as I can, before intertwining my fingers between Daniel and Penelope's. "Everyone keep their eyes open please, and fix your gaze over to my sweet Lou," I say as I nod at the portrait.

"Fuck," I hear Daniel mutter under his breath.

"Loubo, as we are about to take this salty pork into our mouths, I'm constantly reminded how much salty pork you took into your mouth before you passed. I'll never forget that night in El Paso, when it seemed like I could never stop shooting loads—

"Amen!" Daniel says interrupting me.

"Not even fucking close Daniel. Lou, I remember saying to you how there wasn't one single ounce left in my ball sack that night and you smiling at me—before pulling out a rolling pin from underneath the bed and slowly smashing my scrotum like it was a pile of kneaded bread until you flattened it out, managing to uncover one last drop. That drop ended up being Daniel—

"That's not true—

26

"SHUT THE FUCK UP DANIEL! It is true. So as we sit an enjoy this beautiful meal, let's all take a beat and reflect on the *fact* that the same small hands that made this meal, may someday squeeze a beautiful baby boy out of your testicles with an instrument made to cook it."

Penelope looks at me baffled, "But there's no bread on this table?"

"His body is the bread," I say as I look skyward. "To the rock hard body of Christ, we say amen," I nod, still keeping my eyes fixated on the heavens. "Fucking say it Daniel."

"Amen," he says reluctantly as he puts his head down and digs in. "This is delightful dear," he whispers to Penelope, quickly trying to change the subject.

"Thank you. Tandy, the doctor's wife, gave me the recipe after church last Sunday," Penelope says.

"What's wrong with your voice Penelope? It's been like that ever since I got here," I say with an entire mouth full of food.

"Why whatever do you mean?" She asks.

"It sounds really fucking weird. Are you on the spectrum at all?"

She furrows her brow. "I'm sorry, I'm not following. Spectrum?"

"The retard spectrum. Think of it as a ROY G. BIV type of wheel, but for retards," I say casually.

"No, I was actually one of the smartest in my class," she shoots back.

"Why is your speech so slow and delayed? Were you hit with a rock in the back of the head. That's happening *a lot* these days," I motion with my fork.

She looks at Daniel and the two of them burst out laughing. "Honey, I'm not retarded, I'm just southern."

"I don't understand," I say as I sneak a piece of pork off her plate as well.

"Dad, it's an accent. She has a southern *accent*. Everyone from this region talks like that. Remember how the Schlagers talked? This is the female version of that accent."

"Get fucked by the dumpster. That's crazy. Why anyone would deliberately talk like that is mind-altering. It's a good thing you're hot and you can cook. Otherwise people might tie a string around your hand and tell you not to stray too far from the donkey, *dummy*."

She laughed, probably because she knew it was true. The next two hours we ate, drank, and shared a laugh together. It reminded me of dinners I had with Lou and the rest of the kids before they were burned alive. It was nice. Also, I obviously got as close as one could to "shit inside someone else's pants while they're still wearing them" wasted. It had been awhile since I felt like I could relax without looking over my dong for someone trying to kill me.

Penelope was pretty cool too it turns out. She reminded me of Daniel's mom, except with a full cup size smaller tits. I would have strived for bigger if I were Daniel, but whatever, that's his fucking journey. He seemed happy, and for a first wife, she's a solid choice until he upgrades younger at some point. After taking endless bullets for me, he deserves to be content and get his dick sucked on the reg.

As Penelope refills our beers once again, Daniel nudges me when she saunters back into the kitchen. "You want to go share a smoke outside with me for old time sake?"

"I'm perfectly fine sitting right here smoking," I say pointing down to the now forty or so ashed out fags.

"Yeah, Penelope isn't that cool with *me* smoking in the house, so do you mind if we pop out front?"

"I guess. Just out of curiosity, what size men's pants does she wear for you? Thirty-two, thirty-two?" I ask as I punch him in the gooch once more with a chuckle.

He buckles over and falls off the chair onto the floor, writhing in pain as I stand above him and laugh. There's nothing like that old father/son gooch shot. Daniel inhales deeply before mustering out—

"There's something else I want to talk to you about. It involves the woman that brought you here."

I grab his hand and help him up to his feet. He coughs, trying to pop his balls back out of his stomach as he dusts himself off and wipes a tear from his eye. We head out to the front porch and take a nice stretch.

The sky is lit up with the most beautiful stars you've ever seen. Stars so perfectly bright, it makes you wonder how God had time to make people like us. Obviously I'm fucking joking. There is no God and I could give a mouse's shit about the bullshit stars. The only time a real goddamn man should notice stars in this life, is if he gets shot outdoors at night and they're the last things he sees before he dies. Even then, keep it to yourself. I wanted to hear about H-Tubs.

"So, what did you want to talk to me about before your wife makes you go to sleep in pajamas with the feet sewn into them?" I ask as I strike a match off my boot, lighting yet another fag.

"That woman isn't who you think she is, Dad," he says.

"She's not a maid or a cook?" I ask inquisitively.

"Um, actually I don't know—

"Because *that's who I think she is*," I say shaking out the match without offering it to him.

"Yeah, she might be that too, but she's part of a bigger movement that's happening down here in the south."

30

"What do you mean?" I ask as I inhale.

"Well, rumor has it that President Lincoln is going to emancipate the slaves. Harriet has been running them out of the south for years now."

"Yeah, she told me before we shared a screw," I say, thinking back to dat ass.

"You fucked Harriet Tubman?"

"No, we shared a *screw*. You don't fuck a woman like that. She dictates what's going down. Is this why you dragged me out here? To ask me about my sexual conquests? If so, you'd better put the cats to bed, because I'm about to spin you a fucking yarn—

"No Dad, I don't want to hear about the girls you've banged out. I want to know what we're going to do?"

I take another pull of my heater and look into the distance. "Well, according to her, we only have one option; join the Confederate army."

Daniel looks at me visibly upset, "But Dad, that goes against everything I've been doing down here while I was waiting for you."

"Like it or not, you're an outlaw. You want to hide inside this house with a woman a full cup size smaller than your mom, that's your own goddamn business. But the way I see it, if we want this shit to end— the hiding, running through the forest, breaking into houses and wearing their husband's clothes so they don't feel like it's cheating just so you can get a decent meal and some pussy—then we have to enlist."

"I don't think—

"That's the only way we get pardoned, Daniel. The Yankees up North want us dead for what we did to those Marshals. With the Confederate states succeeding from the Union, they're desperate for soldiers right now. They're outnumbered three to one."

He takes a long drag of his smoke and exhales as I look him in the eyes. To my chagrin, he still has the same eager look to help out whenever he can since he was a boy. He'll never be as great as me obviously, but fucking A' man he's compassionate as shit. I can tell how torn he is, so I lean in and grab the back of his head and press it to mine.

"That doesn't mean we can't influence this thing and end it quicker," I say.

"What are you saying?"

"I'm saying that I'll play the part, kill who I'm supposed to kill, but the first opportunity I see to end this thing and move on with my life, I'm taking it. You can't win three on one, so we might as well speed up the process."

Now he smiles, finally getting it. "You want to kill Confederates?"

"If that's what it takes, that's what it takes. I don't hold an allegiance to any side in this life, and you shouldn't either. They'll all try and fuck you in the end."

"And afterward? After this whole thing is done, then what?" Daniel asks.

"I'm leaving and going back out west. It's your choice whether you want to come with me or not. The humidity inside my jeans right now is fucking tropical. I want to go back to California and get out of this bullshit."

"Okay. I want to take Penelope with me. I think she'd like California."

"Yeah, that's fucking rad. Speaking of which, your wife got any hot friends around here or are we just stuck out in the middle of the fucking woods with our dicks in a cotton gin?"

"No choice. Had to stay out of plain sight. Sorry. They'll be some in town tomorrow when we sign up."

I flick my cigarette into the woods and re-gooch him on the way back inside. As I hear his body rolling down the front steps in pain, I double-bird him behind my back, never making eye-contact at him. Classic Saint James. I'm sure he appreciates having a father around again.

"Don't wake me up before one-ish for that bullshit tomorrow. We get there when we get there," I say over my shoulder before removing the portrait of Louretta from off the wall walking back toward a bedroom.

Within seconds of slamming the door behind me, I immediately strip down completely nude and begin to hammer the portrait into the ceiling above the bed. I do a series of toe-touches to loosen up before laying down to begin the time-honored-tradition-spread-eagle-two-handed-basket-weave-jack-sesh. The key to a good nightcap like this is keeping your fingers intertwined and using a consistent pace. You see, even though I'm writing my biography, I still take time out to teach. I'm an amazing human and you're welcome for this moment that I have just provided you.

The following afternoon, I wake up around 2:30pm and walk out to the living room to find Daniel and Penelope staring at me. Neither look particularly happy. I glance over at Daniel and shrug my shoulders and he points to a hole carved into the kitchen wall with the portrait of Louretta hanging above it at eye level. There's grape jelly all over the floor underneath it leading to the ground. I shrug my shoulders sheepishly.

"Night terrors. Sorry about that," I say looking away.

"Night terrors huh? But you expertly carved a hole the size of your dick into the wall somehow?" Daniel asks in disbelief.

"Jesus was a carpenter too, Daniel. You should know that from prayer. Penelope, how about you fire up some breakfast, while I go wash the jelly off my feet?"

She nods reluctantly in anger as Daniel throws his hands up. I see him begin to stuff a sock into the hole in the wall on my way out back to clean up. A huge wad of grape jelly squirts out across the floor as he presses in the sock further.

"Motherfucker! Why did you have to use so much?" He screams out to me.

"I AM WHO I AM DANIEL!"

I'm sure he laughed about it later.

Chapter 3

DON'T YOU STONEWALL ME!

May 1st, 1862
Fredericksburg, Virginia

Riding my steed into town with Daniel next to me felt like not wearing a condom, which is to say it just felt natural. He helped ease my nervousness of heading into a heavily populated area for the first time in a long time. I had traditionally avoided them over the last three years for my own safety. Let's face it, if I went into town, I was going to get drunk. If I was going to get drunk, I was probably going to screw. If I was going to screw, then I was probably going kill. If I was going to kill, then I'd probably end up fucking their dead body. That was just my life at the time.

As we trotted through the streets, I notice a few patrons shoot me a mixture of curious looks of "do I know you" and "did you ball my wife?" The answer is obviously "yes" to both of those questions. I keep my head down as much as possible, as did Daniel.

The town itself is bustling, and luckily no one went out of their way to make a stink. This was the first town with a public outhouse, so people could walk in and shit as they please. You didn't need a quarter or a rake tied to a key. Nope, this town was classy. Even the soldier recruiting building seems legitimately well organized, however there was a long line. Daniel could see the look in my eyes as we tied up our horses outside. He reaches over and grabs my arm.

"Dad, don't freak out over the line and go shooting up the place. Remember, we're keeping a low profile so we can fit in."

"Sure, no problem. I'm super patient and I never mind waiting," I reply as we walk over and casually stand in line.

As I look at these fucking hill-jacks that surround me in line, one thing is immediately clear, I am not one of them. Everyone had a beaver-dip* in their top lip, and most of them are missing teeth. I was in a world full of Schlagers, and I was not happy

---

* Beaver-dip is chewing tobacco that you stuff into your upper gums when the lower ones are shot. You come across a guy with a beaver dip, that's a hardcore disgusting motherfucker who doesn't care about what he looks like to the outside world and has probably never seen a dentist his whole life.

about it. A redneck dude missing all of his top teeth taps me on the shoulder from behind.

"You got any rope on you?" The man asks in a thick southern accent.

"Motherfucker, does it look like I have any rope on me? That's not something a person openly carries, and if I did, it would be fucking noticeable," I say annoyed.

"Sorry. I just been pissin' biscuits all day over how I'm going to get my newborn outta my well. I told my goddamn butler to keep an eye on Jessica during her nap, cause she gets real thirsty," he says licking his lips.

"Wait, *you* have a fucking butler? Don't you have to be rich to have a butler?" I ask taken aback.

The entire line erupts in laughter as another guy interjects. "We all have fucking butlers! Where are you from man?"

More laughter ensues as Daniel nudges me and whispers, "Slavery. I told you. Just laugh and don't say a word."

Outrage overtakes me as I think of Harriet and what she must have gone through. I reach for my gun, but Daniel stops me. As I go to swipe his arm away, I'm bumped from behind by a group of men. Like a coke party at Stevie Nicks' house, this was the last straw. I turn and quick draw my pistol. The whole line retreats, as the group of men who bumped me turn around and draw their pistols.

"You got a fucking problem you need solved?" I ask.

An older man with a huge bushy beard from the middle of the pack turns around and walks out front and center. "Indeed sir. The Union Army does. Do you think you can solve it?"

"Dad, put the gun down," Daniels says through pursed lips.

"I can kill any man, anywhere, at any time. A man like you I can recircumcise and have stuffed back up inside your mother's vag like you were never born," I say.

The redneck with the missing upper row of teeth blurts out, "Buddy, I don't think you understand who this is? That's the goddamn—

"Shut that fishing hole you call a mouth. I don't give a shit who it is. If he's so goddamn important they'd carve him into the side of a mountain."

"Perhaps they will some day if we win this war. You enlisting?" The man with the gray bushy beard asks.

"I'm not standing in this line to get my dick measured," I say sternly.

"Of course not. All the rope has just arrived at the Country Store," he says, trying to make light of the situation.

"Jessica! I'm coming!" screams the redneck who is missing the teeth as he runs down the street.

The man with bushy beard takes a step closer to me. "How about we test your shot out back?"

"Gladly," I say as he smiles.

"Lower your weapons. Everyone from the line join us around by the camp," he says before walking off.

Daniel shakes his head as I holster my gun and head out back with the rest of the men from line. There seems to be genuine awe from what just occurred. For me obviously, this might as well be fucking Secretary's Day.

When we turn the corner behind the back of the building, I see what appears to be some type of tent city. Picture current downtown Los Angeles or any other shitty sanctuary city, with different training obstacles set up off to the side. As we enter, Confederate troops slowly start to walk out of their tents to check out the "newbies". I debate taking off my shirt as I walk by, but I ultimately refrain. I still don't know what the fuck is going on. Finally, the man with the bushy beard stops us.

"Here is good," he says surveying the land.

"Good for what?" I ask.

"To test that shot you were bragging about."

I look around puzzled. "You want me to kill all of these people? I mean, I'm cool with it—

I quick-draw my pistol and aim it at a soldier leaning out of his tent, but the bushy bearded man knocks my arm down at the last second and I discharge my pistol into the ground. This brings every man out of their tent. One dude walks out with his penis on a string like it's some sort of pet iguana. The bushy bearded dude seems amused, and truthfully, I am too.

"Not people. Targets. Start with those bottles down range, then pick off the tin coffee cans that are a little closer," he says as he motions.

"Christ. That's it? I do this in my fucking sleep."

"I got money that says you can't hit 'em all," one soldier calls out in a deep southern accent.

"Me too!" Another soldier shouts out next to him.

"Is there a good whorehouse near here?" I ask the soldiers.

"Yeah, we got a decent one down the road," someone barks out.

"Great I want an entire night of whores and whiskey on you two," I say.

"That's fine, it'll be our pleasure—

"I'm not finished. I want both of you to watch me have sex the entire night inside the room. Since I have to teach you how to shoot today, I might as well teach you how to fuck too."

The entire camp howls in laughter. The bushy bearded man laughs as well and shakes his head. I crack my neck back and forth and examine my surroundings. Time to buttfuck.

"One last thing bush, you a coffee drinker?" I ask the older man.

"Yeah, I've been known to enjoy a cup of joe, why?"

With that statement, I quick draw the pistol on my right hip and begin expertly firing down range picking off the glass bottles and tin cups one by one. One bottle, then one cup. I'm going far to close range one at a time just because I fucking can. When I squeeze the trig on my last bullet from the gun on my right, I toss it and unholster the gun on my left hip and continue firing, crushing target after target.

With one bottle of water and one tin cup left, I spin and spot a burlap sack full of coffee beans hanging from a rope off a wooden post that was being used for bayonnette drills. I blast a hole in the bag, which sends the coffee beans sailing high into the sky. I then shoot the individual beans out of the air one by one, before turning aim on the tin cup. I fire a shot, knocking it backwards over on top of a small fire nearby. Spinning around, I fire my last bullet into the only remaining target, which is the bottle of water. In slow-motion we can see the coffee grinds and the water colliding in mid-air, then simultaneously landing inside the coffee cup now on the fire. I toss my pistol and walk over to grab the cup out of the fire and take a sip. The entire tent city rips up in applause.

"Sorry boys, the coffee is shit. Maybe we should go to war with Columbia?" I ask.

Everyone erupts in laughter as the bushy bearded man claps. The first soldier who made the bet looks at me with vengeance. He pulls out his bayonet and begins to charge at me.

"Never drop your weapons private!" he screams as he sprints over.

Without putting down the coffee, I calmly step aside, and leg sweep him on the way past. He hits the ground with a thud, dropping his bayonet. He stands up and takes a swing at me, which I duck. With a right cross that would put Jack Johnson to sleep—and yes—I mean both the boxer and the shitty singer, I knock the man out cold with one punch and continue to drink my coffee. Loud audible snoring can be heard from the man on the ground. The bushy bearded man walks over, nodding his head impressed.

"Alright, alright, that's enough. What's your name?" He asks inquisitively.

"I'm Saint James Street James, I hate road abbreviations so I pronounce my last name. You?"

"I'm General Stonewall Jackson, pleased to meet you."

"I'm sure it is," I say as I begin to walk away.

"You don't know who I am do you?" He asks.

"No, and I don't care. I heard there's a war going on and I'm here to kill people, that's it. Friendships can wait for sleep away camps after this shit is over."

He lets out a big hearty laugh. "Good! We need more soldiers like you! Join me for a Sunday afternoon brooch and we can get to know each other."

"What the fuck is a brooch?" I ask, stopping in my tracks.

"You've never had a brooch? You'll love it! Follow me," he says with a laugh as he walks out of the camp back toward the main street.

I gather up my guns and reholster them, before walking over to the dude I knocked out on the ground. I slap his face, waking him up a bit. He stares at me through groggy eyes as I lean down and grab the back of his hair pulling his head up off the ground.

"Go back to your tent and sleep it off. You'll need it. You're going to watch me fuck tonight and you need to be well rested," I say before letting go of his head.

I point to his buddy who piped up earlier as well. "You too shitneck. Don't think I forgot about you."

He nods his head in shame as I walk over to my son. "Daniel, you stay here and make some friends. After the display I just put on, there's a lot of fear in these men. Capitalize on it and make yourself known. We'll be able to run shit after I gain the General's trust."

"Where are you guys going?" He asks.

"Fuck if I know, it sounded like he said brunch, but it's hard to tell in that retard accent. You know what else is hard? Trying to figure out if a dude is gay or just from Atlanta. You going to be alright?"

"Yeah, I'll be alright. Don't forget I'm the second best gun behind you if you need me," he says in a self-assured tone.

The eager little boy that I knew is now gone. I may not be happy about him being married, but I'm happy he's a fucking man. Nodding my head, I give him a hint of a smile before walking away to catch up with the General.

As I approach General Jackson, he slings his arm over my shoulder like we're long lost bros. I can smell a hint of pussy on his beard, so I let the arm thing slide. Any man who smells like he just went down on someone within a few hours is okay in my book. It means he's confident and he's not in a rush to get the fuck out of somewhere. Now that I think about about it, I wonder if he doesn't trust me because I don't have a little pussy juice in mine. Now I'm fucking paranoid.

Every man in town stops and tips their hat to the General. I can't help but feel jealous, I was that dude for so long. Goddamnit, I miss that feeling. That rush of power. The thrill of the beave. Only men who have had it know what that truly feels like. The rest of you fuckers reading this will have to live through me, and I'm fine with that. This is my fucking burden. We stop outside a barbershop and he slaps me on the back.

"You ready?" He asks with a smile.

"You want me to get a fucking haircut for enlistment? Motherfucker that isn't happening. I thought we were going to get a whiskey?"

He laughs like a mall Santa on Special K. "We are getting a whiskey, but we're also getting a haircut of a *different kind*. Have you really never enjoyed a brooch?"

"I'm sorry man, are you saying *brunch*?" I ask, still confused.

"Sort of. A brooch is a man's *brunch*," he says slapping my back yet again as we walk in.

The barbers stop cutting hair and nod out of respect for the General as he hangs his hat on a coat hook. I follow suit and hang my hat on the wall as well, while he walks me through a door to the back of the shop. He bends down and knocks twice at the bottom of the door, then stands up. A sliding peephole opens and we see a black man open it. He looks up at us from what must be the floor. Yet another fucking peephole. You think people don't trust your shit today, back then everyone had a motherfucking peephole. *Everyone.*

"Ya'll here to get brooched?" He asks in a southern accent.

"Indeed we are sir," Stonewall says.

The peephole slams shut and the door opens. As I go to take a step forward, Stonewall puts his arm across my chest. I look down and notice a stairwell going straight down into a basement. Who the fuck has a room like this? General Jackson nods at me with a pussy-eating smile.

"You ever hear the phrase 'look before you leap'?" He asks.

"Funny enough, I said that once to a blind man at a Fourth of July rooftop barbeque just before he fell off the ledge. Haven't used it since. We lost a good man that day," I say as I hold my hand over my heart.

The General looks at me startled. "Oh. Well then, just watch your step."

I nod pretending like I give a fuck and head down the stairs. The General slams the door shut behind us as we slowly walk down. This reminds me of Manuel's hidden ayahuaska man cave back in the day. It's a little bit darker, yet inviting. In the middle of the room are two barber chairs facing an old wooden bar with a large mirror behind it. A black bartender, Claude, in his sixties dressed in a suit smiles at us as we walk in.

"Ya'll want a drink, sirs?" He axes us.

"Yes Claude, two of your finest whiskey's please," he says to him as if he's known him for a long time.

Claude pours two glasses as we walk over to the bar. Stonewall bro hugs him with one arm and they pound fists. I find it extremely odd that these men get along due to the current state of war we are in and the circumstances of why we are at war in the first place. Stonewall holds up his glass to toast me.

"To segregation!" he says as he tips his glass toward me.

I cock my head back trying to make sense of this. "Toward Claude, or just in general? Also, is the pun intended?"

"Segregation from us and the rest of those poor assholes upstairs getting regular haircuts! They're not down here getting brooched," he says as he and Claude laugh together.

"I'm still not exactly clear on what a brooch is—

"Cheers!" he screams and we slam our shots back. "Two more while we brooch, Claude."

"Yes sir," Claude says as he pours. "Tiny and Bobo, get out here! We got two fine gentlemen here for their Sunday brooch!"

Claude claps his hands twice as two black midgets in their early thirties walk out with rolling carts carrying shaving accoutrements on top. They are also dressed in little suits as well, same as Claude. As we grab our whiskey, they motion for us to have a seat in the two empty barber chairs. I look over next to me and see the General unbuckling his belt, taking off his pants. He kicks off his boots as well. I'm suddenly blasted by General Stonewall Jackson's dick and balls. He takes a hard seat in the barber chair and exhales deeply, opting to leave his shirt on.

Look, I still don't know what the fuck is going on, but I'm not going to be outmanned by another dude braining down on me. I kick off my boots as well and unsheathe my dong, shaking it hard against my leg, creating a loud thunderclap akin to the home team fans behind the visitor's basket during an NBA free throw. I sit down and take a sip of whiskey, casually looking around.

Once we are seated, the midgets pull out a set of metal stir-ups from underneath the chairs and instruct us to put our legs up inside of them. Stonewall does it without blinking, so I did it too. They slow tilt the barber chairs all the way back until Stonewall and I are looking up at the ceiling. What the fuck is this?

"Claude, why don't you leave the bottle over here, I want to properly enjoy the day off with my new friend," Stonewall calls out toward the heavens.

As I hear his feet shuffling over, I suddenly feel a splash of hot water against my taint, followed by a light waving of a towel. A dollop of shaving cream is then applied to my gooch area and lathered in with tiny hands. I peek around the side of my chair and see the midgets pull out straight razors. As casually as I can, I peer over at Stonewall who has his eyes closed, and a huge smile on his face as his midget lifts up his dick and balls like he's pulling a trout from a river, slightly cradling his package up at an angle.

Meanwhile my midget is having a little tougher of a time, so he applies his elbow underneath my whole gift basket to gain some leverage. They each start slowly shaving our taints, much to the delight of Stonewall. In all my years on this earth, I've never seen a motherfucker more satisfied at anything in this life more than Stonewall Jackson getting his gooch shaved on a Sunday.

"There is nothing like a Sunday brooch," he says.

"I gotta hand it to you General, this is *really fucking nice*. I mean, I've been involved in some high end shit before, but this takes the quadriplegic's cake."

"It's just so goddamn humid down here, that it's nice to have your gerbil catwalk shaved up once a week just to feel rejuvenated again," he bellows.

"I was just saying that to someone the other day. Holy shit it's fucking hot. I've never seen anything like it," I say with a chuckle.

"You're not from around here are you? You a carpetbagger?" He asks.

"No, I don't keep my pubes. They can just sweep them off the floor."

"I meant are you from up north? You don't sound or look like anyone I've seen down south," he says.

"Nope. I'm from out west. California actually."

"What are you doing here?" He asks in a more serious tone.

"Sight-seeing. I was hoping to catch a glimpse of Big Ben."

The General snaps his fingers and suddenly his midget pops up behind me with his straight razor, holding it underneath my throat. A bunch of Stonewall's pubes are still stuck to the razor. It's so fucking close that I can smell it. I look up at his black midget in anger.

"You could have him wipe, Stonewall. I can smell the shit you took an hour ago," I say in disgust.

"Answer my question! What the fuck are you doing here? Are you a spy for the Yankees?"

Since I don't have my guns on me, and the other black midget is still holding up my dick and balls as he continues to shave, I'm out of options. I decide whether to lie or not, ultimately choosing the latter. Mostly for the fact that my midget didn't quit shaving. If he had wanted me dead, he could have sliced me nuts to neck and been done with it by now. I slightly move my neck and try my best to face him.

"I'm not a spy. I'm an outlaw. Also, a sexual Icon, an amateur tobogganist—

"What do you mean you're an outlaw? What did you do?" Stonewall seethes.

"I've killed many men. Three hundred or so Marshals," I say as he stares at me puzzled.

"That's impossible. No one's ever killed that many Marshals," he bristles.

"I'm Saint James Street James for fucksakes. I'm famous as shit. As a matter of fact, do you know what a privilege it is to see my dick and balls right now? There's a goddamn nationwide manhunt for me as we speak."

Claude suddenly walks over to the General. He pulls out the all nude Wanted poster and holds it in front of his face. "I'm sorry Mr. Jackson, he is for real."

The General reclines his chair upward from the ground as Claude hands him the poster. He spins it around so he's now looking down on me. The brain job he's giving me right now is almost unbearable. He squints at the nude poster and then at me for comparison.

"The detail of this drawing is so real and accurate. It's remarkable," he says impressed.

"You know what else is remarkable? The fact that your full-braining me right now and I haven't killed you yet," I bark out at him.

"That's mighty brash of you considering you got a blade to your cock and one to your throat," he says, spreading his legs wider.

"The one at my cock, I'm not worried about. Taking a simple straight razor to my dong would be like trying to chop down a redwood with a garden hoe. As for the one at my throat, you and I both know after shaving a taint like yours, that razor is goddamn near dull at this point," I say trying not to inhale his pube scent.

The General looks at me sternly, then lets out a hellacious belly laugh. He then motions the two midgets to back away. I yank the lever on my barber chair and pull it upward. Stonewall slaps my leg with laughter so hard that my dong bounces up off the chair.

"I don't care if you killed three hundred Marshals. I just need you to kill two million more? The Confederate Army needs more men like you who don't give a fuck!"

"You don't say?" I ask genuinely surprised.

"Yeah, those assholes up north have us outnumbered three to one. Truthfully this war would be over by now, but we're short on man power. I've beaten them in so many battles, they should build statues of me when I'm dead and gone."

"I'm sure people would cherish them forever. Since I'm new to this whole shit, why are you at war in the first place?" I ask, finally feeling comfortable in my surroundings again.

"Well, truthfully, we succeeded from the union initially because they're all a bunch of fucking assholes who believe in industrialization, which means bigger buildings and more taxes.

Hell, there's even a rumor that they want to end the sale of alcohol."

"That will never fucking happen. People would lose every last piece of shit inside their bodies. Can you imagine?" The General and I laugh as the two black midgets walk back over and begin fanning our taints with dry towels.

"Tell me about it. Look, us southerners are simple people. We own farms, we make moonshine, we smoke and grow tobacco—it's just a more slow-paced way of life down here and we love it. The North wants to make this war all about slavery, but there's a lot more to it than that. I mean sure, we own slaves and we're super racist, but there's other shit to it than just that. We can concede ending slavery, but the rest of it will kill our way of life. Could you imagine this beautiful town if every building was owned by the same company?"

"I can actually. It happened to me out west," thinking back.

"So what did you do?"

"I killed every last one them. Every single member of their entire family. I even ripped the roots out of the ground after I destroyed their family tree."

"See, you and me aren't that much different," he says tipping his glass toward me.

"Yeah, besides your level of extreme racism, I guess we really aren't that much different," I say.

"What's your goal in this life?" He asks.

"To be rich and to have sex with as many women as possible. You?"

"Pretty much the same. I also want slaves to literally do everything for me," he says matter-of-factly.

"Yeah man, I totally got that. There really isn't a need to put any more emphasis on that one," I laugh.

He smiles and leans in, "So, are you with me?"

"Yeah, I'll kill some fucking people for you. I don't take orders from anyone, because I'm above it, but if you point me in the right direction, I'll fuck shit up."

"Great!"

He stands up and extends his hand. I take this moment in. Two men, standing damn near cock to cock, now with freshly shaven gooches, as two black midgets stare at us. It's like the great Tom Cochrane says, "Life is a highway." I look him in the eye and shake his hand.

"Now spread your legs," he says with a low whisper.

"What?" I ask, thinking I didn't hear him.

"Open up your gait a little. Widen your stance," he says with a wink.

I reluctantly spread my legs, while both black midgets move in from behind us. They dip their hands in some sort of liquid in a bucket, then cup a small palm size of fluid. In unison, still from behind, they slap our taints from underneath. At first, the sensation burns almost like a smolder, then it gradually cools off into the most wonderful feeling a man could ever have in this world.

"Now lean forward and touch your toes," the General says.

I follow his instructions and I'll be goddamned if we weren't hit with the most perfect plume of talcum powder right between the cheeks. Phenomenal. The General hands me my pants as he starts to put his own back on. After he buckles his belt, he slaps me on the back again and smiles broadly.

"Now *that*, is a fine Sunday brooch. There's nothing like channing the tatum. I'll see you in camp tomorrow!"

With that, he pounds his whiskey and puts his boots back on. Afterward, he drops a few bucks to the gooch barbers and heads out. I sit down in the chair putting my pants and boots back on in silence, not really sure what to think. As I take the last pull of whiskey, I think to myself how much I really need another fucking drink. Also, I want to get the hell out of here. As cool as this whole thing was, this is a weird sitch down here, and the stench is palpable. Walking out, I see Stonewall's midget doing sign language to my midget.

He looks at him really pissed off and says to him in a deaf accent, "That was Saint James Street James? Nigga, why didn't you sign something to me? I just kept shaving. I would've have cut that motherfucker's balls off to get that reward!"

I give him the sign language signal for goodbye, which is simply waving my hand, as I exit the shop. He seemed surprised that I was fluent.

Chapter 4

I DESERVE AN ORGY

I walk through town feeling like I have a little bit more purpose, but I'm not really sure what to think of this fucking war now. On the one hand, the slavery thing is really fucked up. On the other, these people just want to be left the hell alone and not get grinded with taxes for stupid shit. I also understand what he means by industrialization ruining everything. As I look around this quaint little town, I can't help but think if there was the same coffee shop on every corner or some shit like that. What a miserable existence that would be. Wink.

I wander into a saloon and light a heater after ordering another whiskey. Looking around the bar, I notice southerners drinking and laughing, enjoying an easy Sunday afternoon. This is far more sophisticated than the rough and tumble bullshit of the wild west I was living in. The women were elegant, and the men had class. Even the whorehouse was separate and *way* down the street, as to not be an eye sore to the general public. Obviously, I was going there right afterward, but for now I want to enjoy this southern way of life.

I spot a man in his late twenties sitting by himself at a table in the corner near a man playing piano. He seemed important, or maybe just homosexual. The two are often hard to distinguish. Periodically, he'd look around the saloon and then jot something down on a sheet of paper. He'd chuckle to himself, then pour a glass of whiskey out of what appeared to be his own bottle. Looks like I just found my new best friend. Hope he doesn't try to suck my cock.

I stand up and walk over to the table and introduce myself. "My name is Saint James Street James, do you mind if I join you?"

"That depends, did you just say your full name because you hate road abbreviations?" He says without looking up.

"Actually, yes, I did," I say surprised.

The man looks up at me curiously from his notes. "I haven't had a man introduce himself like that to me since Doctor Daniel Drive. My name is Samuel Langhorne Clemens, nice to meet you. Please, by all means, have a seat sir."

"Thank you," I say in an unusually light hearted tone, still feeling the effects of my brooch.

"What brings you over?" He asks.

"You know, I just got a Sunday brooch, and I stopped in for some whiskey before I go whoring later—

"As any man should—

"And I'm curious about the south. There seems to be this laid back attitude here, where everyone seems like they're at a dinner party everywhere you go," I say.

"The gin, as well as people's lips, do flow hand in hand," he says while sipping a drink.

"So why the war? These people seem like they could care less," I say pointing around the bar.

Samuel leans in, "You know, I have the same curiosity as you. That's why I traveled here, so I could observe the atmosphere."

I point down to his notes, "Are you a writer?"

"An aspiring one. I'm taking notes for my first book as we speak. I've been traveling around the country, meeting interesting people like yourself, seeing if I can turn it into a story."

"What's the name of your book?"

"I'm thinking about calling it *The Adventures Of Tom Sawyer*. What do you think?" He asks.

"Sounds like a piece of shit. What do you know about the Confederate Army?" I ask, trying to deflect from having to talk about some dude's fucking probable self-published book.

"I can give you all the knowledge from the two weeks I served in it while I was in Missouri if you want?"

"Please do. Why only two weeks?" I ask.

He moves in closer and drops down to a whisper, "It's all that I could stand. The world is changing, but southerners want to hold on to these older ideals, everything else be damned. What I've learned in my travels is, it's going to change whether they like it or not. Slavery is an old way of life and a mindset that will be abolished some day."

I shake my head and take a sip of whiskey, thinking back to the black deaf midget who almost killed me. Samuel looks at me inquisitively.

"Why, are you thinking about joining?"

"Don't have a choice," I say.

"There's always a choice in this life, hence the—

"I got it Huckleberry. Head west in your travels. Try California, less words," I say with a raised eyebrow, ending the conversation that I'm now bored with.

Jesus that guy was pretentious. I get up as fast as possible and spot the soldier from earlier who I knocked out, walking into the bar. After reaching into my pocket, I drop a few bucks on the table, because he's a writer and will never amount to shit. I also sneeze behind him really loud to make him feel alive again inside for a brief moment.

That fuckboy soldier puts his head down as I approach him, doing his best to look away. Upon closer examination, his eye is damn near swollen shut. He tries his best to avoid one eye contact, but I quickly break the ice and grab his shoulder.

"Hey man, sorry about earlier," I say motioning to his face.

"Yeah man, me too—

"I'm fucking kidding. I'm not sorry about shit. Buy me a whiskey and get ready to watch me fuck. I am on one today!" I say as I motion the bartender over. "The whole bottle please. On this guy. The one who looks like he's squinting through a dirty catcher's mitt."

"Okay sir, coming right up," the bartender says with a chuckle.

"This fucking guy looks like he's half Asian, am I right?" I shout out to the patrons around us, going in for the kill.

The patrons at the bar laugh as the barkeep brings over the bottle of whiskey. I drink straight out of it without offering this gimp-dick any. A bet is a bet. You run your mouth like a steam engine, you're bound to get caught up in the smoke. Man that line was shitty. I'm glad I didn't say that out loud in this moment. It would have really killed the momentum I had going.

"Where's your buddy at? He better not bitch out. I don't want to see him hobbling out of a tent with a watermelon under his shirt, telling me he couldn't come because he's pregnant," I say in disgust.

"What? Has someone actually done that?" He asks puzzled.

"Not only has someone done it, but they actually named the fake baby too and attempted to raise it like a real child. The goddamn thing finally disintegrated into a moldy mess five years later," I say looking off into the distance.

"Jesus. Alright, my buddy will be here in a few minutes. By the way, you know you can't act like that during training. They'll have your ass," he says.

"I don't need training. It's fucks like you I'm worried about," I say taking a full swig off the bottle. "You cross someone like me again, it will cost a lot of people in your unit their lives because of your own bad decisions. There's your pal," I say as I motion for him to come over to the bar. He looks less than enthused as he shuffles over.

"What are your names?" I ask.

"I'm Cyrus and this Bumpy."

"How the fuck did you get the name Bumpy?" I ask the dumpier one.

"I fell off the back of my pa's wagon when we were riding over some rough terrain when I was a kid. Name stuck ever since," he says in a thick southern accent.

"Your parents must have been deep thinkers. Well, you guys ready to watch me fuck?"

"Can we just give you the money and you go to the whorehouse by yourself? We really don't need to be there," Bumpy says.

"Nonsense Bumpy, you do. You called someone out and lost a bet, this is a valuable teaching tool. Plus, it's not often you get a class in sex education from the best to ever swing a twig and pinecones around," I say as I grab my junk.

"Who the hell are you man?" Bumpy asks.

"If you didn't know who I was, you shouldn't have ever called me out today. Let that be a lesson. You never know who anyone *actually* is in this life. One moment you're making a harmless bet, the next you're staring at another man's asshole from behind as he rails a whore, Bumpy."

Suddenly, a stout man in his fifties with a huge white handlebar mustache bursts through the doors holding up my all nude Wanted Poster. The look on his face is one I've seen a hundred times over the past three years; controlled desperation. He's a fucking bounty hunter who has already mentally spent all the money he thinks he's going to take from my head. Not today fuckface. He spots me and crosschecks it with the sketch on the poster and goes for his gun before screaming out—

"Saint James Street James, you're wanted for—

Before he can get out the rest of that sentence, I quick draw my pistol and blow him away. People are genuinely stunned. Again, this isn't the wild west, so this type of shit didn't happen too often inside bars on a Sunday. I look at the two soldiers as if nothing happened.

"So about that whorehouse you were going to pay for?" I say with a smile.

"Right this way, sir," Bumpy says nervously as he hurries us out the front door.

Once outside, Bumpy loses it. "Seriously man, who the hell are you?"

"I'm Saint James Street James, and I'm probably the most wanted man in the United States right now," I say as I light up a heater.

Cyrus stops dead in his tracks. "Wait, you're Saint James Street James? *The* Saint James Street James?"

"You say that as if there is another one somewhere. It'd be unusual to meet another man with four names like myself," I laugh.

"You've killed hundreds of men. You also created the biggest opiate trade on U.S soil. You had sex on top of your dead son's casket. You—

He suddenly stops, wondering if he should say the next sentence, so I complete it for him. "Lost your entire family in a house fire started by Marshals? Yes. I'm that motherfucker."

Both men look down, almost afraid to make eye-contact. "Someday books will be written about me, probably by myself, because I'm the only one who could do myself justice—and when they come out many years after your both dead, only then will the world know the true, raw, sexual, extent of my life. Since that's going to be awhile, cherish the fact that tonight you will have a front row seat to greatness."

"Shit. I'm actually looking forward to this now," Cyrus says.

Bumpy still seems kind of confused. "I'm sorry, it's cool that you're famous and all, but I'm still uncomfortable having to watch you fuck."

"Well Bumpy, you better get over that real goddamn quick, because this shit is about to go down," I say as I take another long pull of whiskey.

Cyrus nods and reluctantly picks up his pace as he leads us to the whorehouse at the end of the street. On the outside, it's nothing special. There's a sign that says **"Chantelle's"** in the same font as the chapter titles on this book. Real fucking original. Walking inside though, it felt like home.

As I breeze through the double doors, that old whorehouse scent hit me smack in the biscuits. You know how people always say that "smell" is the strongest sense we have? It's fucking true. The stink that washed all over me stepping inside this joint was so unmistakable, that I could have told you how many dicks had been inside each girl. It's so distinct, there really is nothing like it. Glade sure as shit couldn't replicate if they tried.

Take a strong inhale and imagine a hundred smoked cigars mixed with twenty semi-warm dirty wash cloths that have been rubbed against every whore's vagina multiple times, and have now been wrung out into a thrice used shot glass filled with cheap whiskey. It's faintly masked by cheap perfume that has been endlessly sprayed after each man has left their makeshift bedroom for the hour. Fuck. I probably went too deep with that. Whatever asshole. Your favorite scent is probably a fucking baseball field or Strawberry Shortcake sleeping bag. This is my sanctuary.

I walk over to the bar where I see a smiling bartender in his late sixties, who I immediately slap across the face. We're in a whorehouse, so he's getting a rap on the beak for the upbeat attitude. Whenever a bartender gives you a look like that inside a place like this, it's like your grandfather telling you to go hit on the older girl in your school for him. It's fucking creepy. Keep an even keel, realize this is a place of business, and not some goddamn strongman contest at the county fair. Don't give me that knowing wink like you've tested the merch and we're about to be Eskimo bros. When I'm about to pump 14 ounces of semen into someone, do you think I want to know that you have too? *Jackass.*

"Pick yourself up and give me a whiskey," I say, eyes fixated on him.

"Yes sir," he says nervously in a thick southern accent.

He grabs a bottle and sets it down in front of me, and I backhand him again, slapping him to the ground once more. Cyrus and Bumpy look on in shock, as the bartender peers up at me from the floor. I cock my head sideways and glare at him, while sliding the bottle over in front of Bumpy.

"This isn't my first whorehouse, so I'll be goddamned if you're going to give me the well whiskey that you've poured inside the expensive bottle after everyone is gone. My friends might be fine with it because they've always been poor and don't know any better, but I want the good shit you got stashed away underneath the floorboards," I demand.

"But I don't—," he weakly musters.

"NOW SLAPDICK," I say raising my voice to the pitch and tone one is accustomed to hearing right before they might get killed.

He shakes his head furiously, as he scrambles to find the crow bar underneath the bar to pop the floor boards up. Once he has it, you can see the slits that have been made where the wood is worn as if he's done this a million times after hours. Cyrus and Bumpy stare at me incredulously, obviously in awe of my whorehouse prowess.

After a half-hearted attempt to pretend as if he's never popped the floor boards, the wood rises with ease—much to his humiliation—revealing a bottle of whiskey as old as his grand pappy's skull. He pours one of the smoothest shots I've ever had. This shit was so aged, it was as if it was stirred with Christopher Columbus' dick on the bow of the *Pinta* once he hit land.

"I'll take your finest whores, chief," I say with the complete calm of a salt water lake.

"You want me to get Chantelle for you?" He asks.

This time I give my other backhand a workout, as I strike him back down to the ground. He holds his face in pain and looks up at me again with the shock of a single mother pulling a chainsaw out of her kid's Halloween bag. I shake my head in disappointment.

"No Cleatus, or whatever the fuck your name is, I don't want the fucking girl with her name on the sign outside. You know how loose that vag is? Every Lonzo, LaMelo, and LiAngelo that has been through here wants to fuck the owner thinking they're going to give her the best screw of her life. Hell, most of them thought they might even be able to change her. Possibly take her out of this town and get her to settle down with the one dick she just couldn't resist. Come on man. You and I know full fucking well that snatch is so spacious that we could fight the rest of the Civil War inside that goddamn thing."

"So what are you looking for?" He asks with measured seriousness.

"I'm looking for the coin purse brother, not the whole fucking duffle bag. Line them up!" I shout as I clap my hands twice.

The bartender nods and puts two fingers in his mouth and whistles. Women of all shapes and ages appear from various rooms, some leaning down looking over the railing on the second floor. The whorehouse turns quiet, men and women, knowing something magical is about to happen. You can tell they have never seen an experienced whore wrangler like myself around these parts. Everyone looks on with intrigue like I'm the ringleader at the fucking circus.

Feeling the need to put on a show to further establish my dominance, I take a few steps out from the bar toward the center of the saloon, and spin on my heels slowly as I survey the women. I eye them up and down, carefully studying their looks and disposition. A fat needy one starts waving at me immediately like a child waves to their parents as they pass by on a Ferris wheel to prove that they're having fun. Obviously she's fucking OUT. I lock eyes with her to let her know adequately.

"You knew you wouldn't make the cut right?" I ask her.

"Yup. Sure did. I'm gonna head back in and finish jacking this dude off in a scarecrow outfit," she says quickly as she disappears back into a bedroom.

The woman that was to her left flashes me her beaver by sliding her panties over to one side underneath her dress. I wave my finger at her like Dikembe Mutumbo. You're not driving into this paint tonight.

"Come on. You see boys, she's telegraphing it. If she's throwing beave at me this early in the game, that must be her go to move. That means I'm not special enough for something original or spontaneous," I say as other men nod to themselves.

Many men fall victim to a middle finger "electric panty slide to the side". I'm sure she's been filled with more meat than a crockpot in the parking lot at Lambeau Field on Sundays. Not this bratwurst. *She gone.*

"Now the woman to her left is interesting. Not a lot of eye contact, and she has a Derringer strapped to the back of her calf, which means she's seen some shit. Unfortunately, it looks like it's been discharged one too many times for my liking. Whatever shit she's seen has obviously haunted her, and therefore she's not about to get weird enough for me. She's looking for your simple basic sex, a 'quick jam' as they say in the biz, then she wants you on your way. No finger in the ass, no spanking. Sorry sister," I say as I give her the thumb out of here.

The whore smiles with respect as she leaves. Chantelle herself has now walked out, looking and sounding exactly like you think she would. She's got the cadence down of how to properly time those high heels to click across the old floor boards she's trotted on a thousand times before to grab men's attention. She smiles and lights up a cigarette.

"How about a ride on a horse you can trust?" She asks with a put on accent.

"Oh Chantelle, I applaud the effort," I say as I begin to slow clap. "You really play the part, and that's a lost art form. I do enjoy an old fashioned whorehouse owner who loves her work. There's a sense of pride in that, and I appreciate it."

Bumpy looks like he's going to cream his fucking jeans over her and is astonished that I haven't said yes to the dress. "Why not her? She's incredible."

73

"You're blinded by ignorance Bumpy. She's older than she looks, late thirties/early forties, she's really fighting for every last year of youth. If you're looking to get mothered before, during, and after sex—she's your gal. She'll tell you that you did a great job and might even tuck your dick back inside your pants for you after you're done. A normal man would walk out of her room with a pep in his step, feeling like he just hiked Mount Kilimanjaro—

As soon as that sentence escapes my mouth, a portly man who is balding early in life walks out of her room smiling like Jack Nicholson as *The Joker*. The room roars with laughter. The guy looks around confused, not sure what's going on, before quickly leaving. Chantelle curtsies, bowing out, but most likely headed to grab the cash off the nightstand.

"Now the girl just to the right of where Chantelle was is exactly my brand of smokes. We have our first contestant. Early twenties, big enough tits with no bruising, she isn't smoking a cigarette, and definitely wants to get out of here. I'm guessing she's from a small town and didn't enjoy the farm life, or the three men in it. She's not here for the long haul, she'll make some lucky fuck her husband and control him with her pussy forever because she can," I say with a wink.

"What do you mean by tits with no bruising?" Cyrus asks.

"Women with huge tits in a whorehouse usually encourage biting or a quick slap. They know where their money is being made and why they are chosen, therefore those tiddies are going to suffer a little wear and tear. My lady, come on over," I say as I motion to her with my index finger.

As she walks over, she smiles at me seductively never breaking eye contact. "She sees there's no ring on this finger, and she might just be walking out with a husband after all," I say to the crowd.

"It would be my pleasure—

I cut her off before she can finish the sentence. "I'm kidding. You still work at whorehouse and I physically and mentally know that, therefore I would never ask for your hand in anything other than jacking me off."

"Understood," she says with a twinge of disappointment.

"Now for the next mistress of the night," I say taking a swig of whiskey.

I scan the room and spot a dark haired girl with olive skin in her late twenties. She looks inviting, yet mysterious. I nod towards her.

"I'll take you," I say with confidence.

"Why her?" Bumpy asks.

"This one is a natural beauty, not a lot of make-up. She's confident in her looks and also doesn't have time for it. A lot of people mistake you for Italian, am I right?"

"Yes. Or a Spainard," she says.

"But the truth is, you're neither. My guess is Native American, but you haven't told anyone. Don't worry your teepee is safe with me, there's no more land to take on this coast from what I hear," I say flashing a warm smile.

This draws more elicit laughter from the bar. There really is nothing like casual racism to bring the true spirit of the Confederates together. It's almost too easy. She looks away coyly, still not answering the question.

"Native Americans are the best lovers. They're crazy and creative in bed. I know, I was raped by twenty of them as a boy. Best night of my life. That being said, you need at least one girl in the orgy who is willing to take things to the next level. Someone to encourage light to heavy choking in some instances, or just jump through the fucking window right at the peak of orgasm to heighten your fear. The enjuns do shit right in the bedroom."

Every man nods in agreement.

"Now for the last one, and yes, I'm stopping at three. Any man worth his own ball weight will tell you that anything more than three on one, someone is leaving unsatisfied. If you're looking to dip your quill in more ink than that, switch the event to a formal swinger's party where the activity is in a more controlled environment."

Bumpy looks at Cyrus dumfounded. "This is a master class in excellence."

In the corner of the saloon, I see a shorter woman with rather small breasts. When I point to her, she seems genuinely shocked and excited. She tries to suppress her smile, but is unable to.

The bartender shakes his head perplexed. "Why her? I mean she's one of the least chosen we have—

I peel off yet another backhand across his face and he hits the floor again. "You're a barkeep man, know your place and shut the fuck up."

"YES! SHUT YOUR FUCKING MOUTH BARKEEP!" a fat man screams out from a front table near the bar.

As the last woman approaches me, I hold up my index finger as she leans in to kiss my cheek. "Can you remove your boots ma'am?"

"Sure," she says as she looks at me intrigued.

She removes her boots, and as her bare feet hit the floor, we see that she is now another three to four inches shorter. At 6'3", I tower over her. I pat her on the head and lean down to truly emphasize my point.

"What are you, five feet at best?" I ask.

"I'm actually five feet even," she says nervously.

"You *have* to say that. The legal maximum height for a midget is 4'11", and a midget prostitute is a specialty, seldom requested in a whorehouse. You'd never be able to make a proper living. If you weren't here, you would be giving brooches down the street, correct?"

"That or testing out throw blankets to make sure they're not *too* big," she says with a look as if she's had that gig before.

I pat her on the head and turn back toward the crowd. "You see, with a short girl, not only does she already look up to me, but she also has a low center of gravity making her difficult to topple over. With four in a bed, there's an excessive amount of movement and lot of space being taken up. The height and weight of every participant must be considered when having a proper orgy on a bed. This wee little one completes the perfect whorehouse orgy."

Every man and woman stands and gives me a rapturous ovation. It's much deserved to be quite honest. What I do is a science, and I deserve to be lauded for it. I also deserve this orgy that's about to go down. It's been awhile. I motion for Bumpy and Cyrus to follow me into a back bedroom, as well as Chantelle the owner who has now popped back out as she counts her money.

"You want me to watch?" She asks, somewhat honored.

"Yes. And to also provide a detailed play-by-play to these two soft shits," I say motioning to Cyrus and Bumpy. "Some of these moves will probably need to be explained, like when I go full Pangea—

"Where all of you are joined as one," she says knowingly.

"Precisely. I don't want to stop and take the time to explain. It's disrespectful to the sanctity of the orgy. Treat them as if they are blind children inside a fly-fishing store."

"Understood. After you Mr. Street James," she says guiding us toward a larger bedroom reserved for groups of five+.

Chapter 5

I'M RAD AT WAR

Around 6am the following morning I walk out of the whorehouse shirtless, with a towel around my neck, holding a damn near empty bottle of whiskey. I'm sweating like Ali at the end of *Thrilla In Manila*. My dick went the full fifteen rounds, and it ended in a stunning TKO. Behind me, every whore and patron has slowly walked out front to pay their respects in a Shia Labeuf trance-like applause. I give a Judd Nelson *Breakfast Club* air fist without turning around. In the distance I can hear Chantelle talking to some of the other whores.

"There goes Saint James Street James, the best there ever was," she says through a choked up voice, fighting back tears.

Some of the shopkeepers who are sweeping out in front of their stores getting ready to start the day, tip their hats toward me in admiration. One by one they each take their brooms and flip them upside down and begin stomping the handles against the wooden steps in appreciation for what I have just given. I tip my hat back out of respect for the recognition. I left it all in the bed last night.

As I enter the camp town, I see the Confederate soldiers—including Daniel—perfectly lined up, marching together. We make eye contact and he shakes his head. I mouth the word "whorehouse" to him, followed by me loudly shouting—

"I JUST FUCKED THREE WOMEN AT THE SAME TIME DANIEL!"

Daniel puts his head down in embarrassment as some of the soldiers try not to chuckle. General Stonewall Jackson walks out of his tent with a curious look as to what the commotion is all about. He squints his eyes in my direction.

"Are you joining us for drill this morning Mr. Street James?" He asks.

"Not a goddamn prayer. I'm going to catch a few winks and try and shake this off. I'll try and pop out around the two-ish region if I can, but I wouldn't be expecting it," I say as I take the last swig of my whiskey.

After downing it, I chuck the bottle high into the air, and without looking at it, I cavalry draw, and blow that motherfucker to pieces. I stumble into to the closest tent near me and fall in, landing on something uncomfortable. Barely able to roll over, I reach into my pants pocket and pull out a perfectly carved to scale totem pole of my cock that the Indian chick sculpted for me during some point of our love-making. I told you, those Indians are fucking mysterious. I stand it up on the ground beside me before passing out.

Ten hours later, I'm awakened by Daniel, who is kneeling over me—shaking the shit out of me.

"Dad, wake up, it's half past four in the afternoon—is that your dick?" He asks, staring at the statue.

"I open my eyes and come to life. The light peeking through the tent felt good on my face."

"Hey Dad, you're just speaking to me in descriptive sentences about what you're actually going through right now," Daniel says quietly.

"Oh fuck. I was? Sorry about that. Yes, that's my fucking dick. Is there any dinner around here? I need some meat in the ole' mouth hole," I say pointing to my chompers.

"Yeah, we're about to break for chow. General Jackson is pissed. You can't miss regiment anymore. He pulled me aside and

83

said he can't show you any favoritism in front of the other soldiers," Daniel says.

"Fuck him. What about those other two dudes I boned in front of? Did they show up?" I ask.

"Yeah, they suffered through it. Said they didn't want the General's wrath. They also said you fucked three women for over eight hours straight," he says as he shakes his head in *belief*.

"It was probably closer to nine, but if that makes them feel better about their lives, so be it," I say.

"Dad, the other soldiers are asking a lot of questions about you. You're definitely not laying low like we talked about."

"I am who I am Daniel," I say as I hand him the dick totem pole. I squeeze his fingers around it, so he definitely knows I'm different.

"Dad, I don't want your dick—

"Stop. You do. If something ever happens to me, I want you to remember me for who I really was. Now, let's go get some dinner," I say before leaving the tent.

Daniel and I stand in the line of soldiers waiting to get fed. Again, I *really* love lines and have a ton of patience, so this is super fucking fun. Daniel pre-emptively grabs my arm knowing that I'm about to cut this shit. Bumpy suddenly appears from the front and hands me a plate of food.

"Here you go Mr. Street James," he says as he hands me a meal.

"What's this for? Is there cyanide in this? If so, I want you to know I'm immune to it," I bristle.

"No, I just wanted to thank you for last night. What you did in there was truly awe-inspiring. I even decided to change my name back to my real birth name. You're looking at a new man. No more Bumpy Jones for me anymore."

"Oh yeah? What is your real name?" I ask.

"Tumultuous Jones. See you at the camp fire," he says as he shakes my hand and walks off.

I turn to Daniel. "I'm pretty sure he doesn't even understand the irony of that. Oh well, have fun in this line. I'm going to pop on down to the camp fire, I'm fucking starving," I say as I pat him on the shoulder and leave him standing in the long line that I still can't see the front of.

As I stuff my face like I just won a challenge on *Survivor*, I take a seat on a big log around the campfire with the rest of the soldiers. I'm getting a lot of looks thrown my way, but no one is really saying anything. The only thing breaking up the chomping of food by people missing half their teeth is a young man playing a banjo in front of the fire with half of his thumb cut off. I decide not to ask how it happened knowing it was some backwoods shit, and instead get up and join him.

"You played the jo' for awhile?" I ask.

"Yes sir. This was the only thing my Pa left me after he went to the war and lost his life. I've played it every night since," he says earnestly.

"Well, it sounds really shitty. Or maybe it's just out of tune. I can't tell until I lay my digits on it. You want to hand it over to the big guy who still has the full ten and slide the fuck down? I'm a professional," I say as I wiggle all ten of my fingers in front of his face. So much for not saying shit.

He looks at me strange before reluctantly giving me his banjo. I retune it in a matter of seconds and shake my head in disappointment, not understanding what this fucking guy couldn't hear. Once I've settled on the proper key, I pull a few finger picks out of my jacket and attach them to my tips. I look out at the soldiers who have now gathered around. Most of them give me salty looks, and I can feel their resentment from earlier. Time to make amends with the old jo'. Goddamnit how it heals fresh wounds.

"This is a song I wrote called *Hiding The Corn Cobb At Tilda's*. Mike Will made it," I say as I bow my head, respecting the jo'.

I tear into the most, raw, honest, twenty-two-minute acoustic version of *Hiding The Corn Cobb At Tilda's* that you've ever heard. The soldiers are dancing like I'm playing *Runaway Jim* at a Phish concert on New Year's Eve, each of them becoming more and more entranced in the music following each and every pick of the jo'. The boy whose banjo I took looks at me like I'm playing a foreign object, leading him to have a full blown epileptic seizure on the ground. I let him continue without calling over medical attention. This is his moment, and I respect it.

Towards the end of my jam, I see Daniel finally walk over with a plate of food. We lock eyes, and all I think is—fuck man— he waited in that line for twenty-two minutes? I would have flipped my shit. Good on him though. Next to him I see General Jackson walk over and starting nodding his head in appreciation for my musical gifts. I stand up toward the end the song and start playing the banjo behind my back. When I'm done, I hold the banjo by the neck and dip it into the fire, igniting it. As it goes up in flames, I bash it into the ground over and over and over again. The fucking thing shatters everywhere and the soldiers go bugfuck. I fall to my knees and hold what remains of the banjo neck above my head, soaking in the energy.

As the applause rains down, I look over and see that someone has given a cup of orange juice to the kid who just finished having a seizure. I walk over and pat him on the head, then lay the burned remains of the banjo in his lap. He looks down at the smoldering neck and then looks back up at me with tears in his eyes.

"Tha-tha-that was incredible," he says with a slight stutter.

"What you heard was a *real* musician," I say.

"Maybe I can be as good as you someday," he musters out.

"Now that would be something—considering what appears to be a newfound disability that you have. But with hard work and determination—

"I control my destiny," he says with a smile, completing my sentence.

"That's right. You sure are—OH FUCK!"

KABOOM!

A cannonball fires straight into his chest from overhead, killing him instantly. The entire camp scurries back to their tents to grab their weapons. I reach down and grab this kid's gun, because let's face it, he's not going to need it. With his weapon now in hand, I sprint over to Daniel.

"They're coming in from the North! No pun intended!" General Jackson screams out. "Everyone grab your bayonets and follow me!"

I grab Daniel by the shoulders and smile at him. "You ready to go fuck shit up with your old man again just like old times?"

"Let's do it," he says excitedly.

Daniel grabs his gun and we follow the charge out of the campsite through town and up toward the mountain ridge. One by one, Daniel and I keep blowing motherfuckers away, simply for the fact that we can. There are no black people fighting, so fuck it. Being able to legally kill without any repercussion feels pretty goddamn awesome. How often do you get to do shit like this? Once every thirty years, maybe? I *really* can't overstate how much I enjoyed this.

You want to talk about some good old fashioned father/son time, this was the ultimate. There's nothing like blasting people in the face side by side next to your boy. The laughter we shared after caving these dudes heads in was unabashed. It was just pure fucking freedom. I mean, sure, the reload on these piece of shit bayonets sucked. It's exactly what you see in the movie *Glory*. But if a reload failed, you could just run at them and stab people in the heart. It was so great. Why can't we do shit like this today? What I wouldn't pay to go back.

Anywho, this battle lasted about three or four days, then those fucking pussies gave up. Years later, people who suck each other's dicks while wearing glasses—historians—would name it "The Battle Of Fredericksburg". Real fucking creative. To me, those days will always be known as the "Please Stop, I'm Bleeding Real Fucking Bad, I Beg Of You Not To Kill Me Battle".

No matter what you called it, that was the best form of bonding I could have asked for with Daniel. This is when I really got to know my son again. For the first time in my life, I just went wherever I was told, because I got to hang out with him.

After all, I knew no one was ever really going to say shit or get in my face because of how devastating I was on the battlefield. It's funny how much the Wild West mentality translated over here. To be honest, it was a little more passive on this side of the country. There still weren't any rules out there, where as here in a fully formed union of states, you had nothing but rules.

As the days and months passed, we marched through Virginia, continuing to fuck shit up together. We'd kill a bunch a dudes, fuck a bunch of women, and then burn down their houses. Turns out, burning down people's shit was a big thing here. No wonder those motherfuckers did it to me. This was one of their main tactics. It's a little bitch-like for my taste. If you want to kill a dude, look him in the fucking eyes, don't burn down his shit. Whatever. Like I said, I didn't really give a shit about the war, so I went along with it. As soon as I could find a way out of my sitch, I was going to bounce.

The Confederates did throw rad parties though. On New Year's Eve of 1862, General Robert E. Lee rolled in for this "End Of The World" party they were throwing. Why did they call it "The End Of The World" party? Well, the *Emancipation Proclamation* that President Lincoln had signed was about to kick in on January 1st, 1863—so these motherfuckers were going off one last time. You want to talk about raging, Robert E. Lee, aka

Fast Eddie, could drink with the best of them. And he was not afraid to pull his dick out and throw down. *Literally.*

Since Lincoln had already signed this bill on September 22nd of this year, people knew this was going down for awhile, but General Lee thought he would have won by now—deeming the bill useless. Needless to say, the war was still dragging on, and he was fucking lit by the time he showed up at this southern mansion party.

To this day, this was one of the best parties I've ever been to. I don't give a baker's fuck that they didn't have indoor plumbing either. Matter of fact, that's probably one of the things that added to the rowdiness of it. The line at the outhouse was long, and you could see grown women hiking up their dresses, pissing all over the front lawn. Men were taking shits in the bushes. No. One. Fucking. Cared.

Daniel and I were inside hitting on two twins in their early twenties, when Fast Eddie comes stomping up. He points at Daniel and asks him for a drink. I don't like his tone immediately and I could tell he was fucking rocked, but I nod at Daniel to pour him a glass of whiskey. Daniel obliges, but Robert E. Lee, takes off his glove and slaps him with it.

"I wanted a glass of whiskey, not a shot. Do better," he barks in a thick southern accent.

Obviously, I'm not putting up with this shit, so I backhand him to the floor. He looks up at me stunned as I stand over him. "He's not the fucking barkeep. If you want more than the half glass like he poured, then you should have asked for the whole goddamn bottle, you old bag of shit."

The party halts to a stop as he defiantly stands up and gets in my face. "What did you say to me, boy?"

"I'm not your fucking son, and I'm certainly not going to tap dance for you if that's your next question, so don't call me 'boy'. You hear me?" I say sternly.

"I'm General Robert Edgar Lee and you will not talk to me like that private," he says as he pokes my chest and drops his right hand down toward his pistol.

I smile and pull out my dick, tucking a cigar underneath my shaft and above my balls, making it look humanistic. "Not only will I talk to you like that, my *private* will as well."

With the skill of a master level ventriloquist, I begin to make my dick talk to him without moving my lips whatsoever. "Saint James Street James will kill you old man. I'd apologize and walk away," I make my dick say, throwing my voice.

The party laughs in unison at Robert, which enrages him. He draws his pistol, and I smack it away. A bullet ricochets off a metal pot in the kitchen, then flies back toward me, taking the

92

end off my cigar. I quickly light it and make my dick talk back to him.

"Thanks Cornnuts. That cigar was way too long to get a proper inhale," I make my dick say.

As the smoke rises into his face, he immediately begins coughing. The laughter only increases at the party. He's so fired up that he lunges at me with two hands, trying to choke me. Stonewall Jackson races in and prevents him from laying hands on me. My dick and balls are still out by the way. I definitely want you to know that I didn't put them away, even as a gunfight was escalating.

"Sir, you don't want to do this. He and his son are our two best soldiers out on the battlefield," Stonewall says to Robert.

"This man is mocking me! I am the leader of the Confederate Army for Christ sakes! I want him dead!" Robert E. Lee screams.

"Eddie, you can't beat him in a gunfight. Trust me. Perhaps there is another way? You are a distinct purveyor of whiskey are you not?" Stonewall asks.

"There isn't a man I can't outdrink! Shots!" General Lee declares.

A black bartender in his mid-fifties, begins lining up shots on the bar. Six a piece to be exact. The party starts to gather around us. This smirking son of a bitch stares me down like he's going to win this. He tugs on his waist band and walks around me in a circle, hemming and hawing, really putting on a fucking show. I zip up my pants and retuck, now that it's game time. I've got to put this motherfucker in his place.

"Shall we bet on this on how fast we can drink them?" I ask.

"Indeed we shall! What do you have in mind?" Lee challenges.

"If I win, bartender gets to go home for the evening and you serve us drinks the rest of the night," I say loud enough for everyone to hear.

He looks at me appalled. I knew this would fucking burn him. "You're kidding. You want to give a slave the night off work? Now why and the Sam Hill do you want to do that?"

"With the Emancipation taking effect tomorrow, I'm sure he'd like to go home and celebrate with his family. I'm a man who can separate war and historical significance. After all, it is New Year's Eve, and you can't battle *every* night."

He points at the slave. "That man isn't worthy to lick the bottom of my boots!"

"But I am. So if I lose, not only will I lick the bottom of your boots in front of all these fine people, but I'll drink the rest of this bottle of whiskey *out of your boot*," I say, as the crowd groans in delight.

General Lee is cornered now and he has no choice but to accept. "I've marched twelve miles in these boots today alone, and I wouldn't wish that disgustingness upon any man... *except you. You're on!"*

Got heem.

"Shall we sir?" I ask as dignified as I can.

Robert E. Lee walks over to the bar with me and puts his arm on my shoulder. Through gritted teeth he whispers, "I'm going to stay and watch until every last drop is gone from my boot. I want it bone dry by the end."

I force a laugh and wink at the bartender. "Pour this shit!"

General Lee looks down at the shots, then over at me with a more serious look to him. "Count it down," he says to the bartender.

"Three, two, one— go!" the bartender says.

With the party intently watching, I pound all six shots, slamming down each glass, before he can get through his third. I then take the bottle that is half empty and chug that too, finishing up just as he is finishing his last shot. I slam the empty bottle down at the exact same time he slams down his last shot glass. General Lee is fucking pissed. He grabs the bartender by his jacket.

"You're not going anywhere!" he says as he staggers backwards.

And that's when the whiskey hits him. This isn't going to be good. General Lee turns to his wife and vomits all over the front of her dress. He's like a human fire hose. Every square inch of the front of her dress is covered in bits of sick and mess. After about forty-five strong seconds, he finally manages to stop.

Wiping his mouth on his Confederate coat, he leans over to me. "The south will rise *ablahhhhhhhh*—

He can't even get the rest of the words out. Instead he staggers backward again and begins hucking all over the *back* of his wife's dress. It's just as violent and every bit as disgusting as when he sprayed her down the first time. I've never seen that much liquid come out of a human being before. General Lee tries to talk but is unable too. He's like a prizefighter who is knocked unconscious and trying to pick himself up off the canvas, but he has no sustainability in his legs and he starts moving sideways— slamming hard into the wall. Lee reaches for a curtain to hold himself up, but the curtain is too long. Instead, he falls right out the fucking window on to the front porch.

"Jesus Eddie. Get ahold of yourself man," Stonewall says in disgust.

"If you'll excuse me," Mrs. Lee says as she tries to hold back tears, covered in her husband's sick.

She walks out the front door as fast as she can. The party looks out the broken window, where we now see the General stand up and fall backward off the porch into a set of bushes. He grabs a fistful of shrubs to pull himself up, but immediately starts puking again. People try to look away, but it's like a goddamn car crash. Sensing that we're losing the party and I haven't boned yet, I hop behind the bar.

"Who wants a drink? It looks like I'm bartending tonight!" I yell out.

The crowd cheers, finally moving away from the window. I lean over to the bartender and shake his hand. "Enjoy the night. I got this."

"Sir, I can't let you do this," he says.

I pull my time piece out of my pocket and hold it up. "It is now exactly midnight, which means it's January 1st. The law says you are free. Happy New Year's."

He smiles, "But sir—

"Get the hell out of here before he gets up and tries to puke on *you*," I say with a smile.

The bartender nods. "Thank you, sir."

He shakes my hand and exits, as two classic southern belles approach the bar. One with a huge set of tits leans over and grabs my left hand. She smiles sweetly as she strokes my empty ring finger.

"I do declare. How is a man like you not married?" She asks in a southern accent thicker than Nikki Minaj.

"Wife got burned up in a house fire. Absolutely incinerated. I'm afraid it's just me and my big dumb giant dick in this world," I say as I look off into the distance for affect.

She leans in even closer, intrigued. "That's terrible. Are you looking for a place to rest your head this evening?"

"I'm looking for a place to rest my whole fucking body. They got us in these piece of shit tents out in the fucking woods."

"Well, that's no place for a man of your stature to sleep on New Year's. I believe I have a bed for you to fill," she says seductively.

"Well, then I do believe I have a warm hole or three I can fill for you," I say.

I can see her counting to three on her fingers, but she's stuck on two. I whistle and twirl my finger, indicating the national sign language symbol for "in the butt". Shhhhh, I told you I was fluent. She laughs and pretends she's not into it, but I can tell she fucking rages. I pour her a drink and the party suddenly comes back to life.

You could tell there was something different in the air this New Year's, that change was happening. Not only was slavery ending, but I was going to have anal sex, which was an extremely rare thing for this time period. In all seriousness, it was an exciting time to be a part of, even if I didn't care about these people's fucking war. You got the sense most of them really

98

didn't care about slavery ending all that much either. There was a lot of fucking media hype, but most people wanted it over with any way.

A few hours later, after my eighteenth drink, I left with the large breasted woman chucking up a deuce sign to Daniel on my way out. He gave me the classic "atta boy" wink that future generations of Brads and Chads have mastered. As I was lifting her up on to my steed outside, she squinted off into the distance, and a look of extreme disgust came over her. I hear a man grunting violently, so I draw my pistol and turn.

"Oh. My. God," the southern belle says.

I take a few steps toward the grunting noises and see Robert E. Lee with his pants down around his ankles taking a shit in the middle of the front lawn. He's completely hammered still, dropping a hard deuce into the snow. Clumsily, he stumbles over to a flag pole and slowly lowers the Confederate flag. Once it's within reach, he rips it in half and begins wiping his ass with it.

To me, that was the defining moment of the war. So much for the south rising again. He fell over hard into the snow with his pants still down around his ankles as I rode off. Best. New. Year's. Party. Ever.

Chapter 6

FOUR SCORE AND SEVEN WHORES AGO

There's nothing worse than walking out of a girl's house hungover as shit into the snow on New Year's Day. It's colder than an aluminum dildo on a metal park bench in Siberia right now. This broad made me a Cornish game hen for the road, but it's going to be frozen solid by the time I actually get to eat the goddamn thing. I rip off a branch from a tree in her front yard and stick it into the hen, before slinging it over my shoulder and hopping onto to my steed. A window on the second floor slams open, and I turn to see the huge breasted woman waving at me, still topless. Her nipples instantly harden from the chill in the air. She knew exactly what the fuck she was doing with that move.

"Write to me while you're at war, okay?" She asks wistfully.

"Nope. I'd rather spend my down time drinking. You understand. War is hell and all that bullshit," I say as I veer my steed toward the main road.

"What if you've left me with child? Don't you want to—

"Not a prayer. Womb to woods. Way to ruin a morning you fucking downer," I say as I shake my head and ride off.

Knowing that she's still watching, I take the stick with Cornish game hen on it and feed it to my horse on the way out. It's like two bites for him, which is hilarious. Plus, that shit would have been so cold by the time I got back to camp that I would have had to start a fire to reheat it. Christ that was annoying about this era. When you were hungry, besides fruit and nuts, everything took fucking hours to cook. That's why everyone looked like starving poor people when they ate, *because you were literally fucking starving by the time you could eat.*

With The Emancipation Proclamation fully kicked in abolishing slavery, this pissed off the Confederates to no fucking end, and the war picked up pretty drastically after this. I'm fucking over it, and truthfully, I just want to head back west. No more winters, no more humidity, and most importantly—no more fucking rules. It was fun while it lasted, but marching all over the fucking country got real old. I'd rather just kill people in my own backyard or at a whorehouse.

With the novelty of war quickly starting to fade for me, I wanted out at any fucking cost. As winter was turning to spring in 1863 and the weather heated up, I pulled Daniel aside from chow one night and sit him down away from everyone, so we can chat in private. A few of the other soldiers played instruments softly in the background.

"You never eat with me. Aren't you going to go play?" He asks, motioning toward the band.

"Daniel, it's not about me. I'm only one man up there playing my heart out every single day, wearing it on my sleeve like a cufflink. I can't give them everything inside me every night," I say as I motion to the soldiers.

Daniel looks at me confused. "Okay, then what are we doing here?"

"I'm going to kill Stonewall Jackson."

"WHAT?!!" He asks in utter shock.

I grab his mouth to cover it, and wiggle a finger inside of it just to freak him out. "Keep your fucking lady voice down and use your inside voice. Max length three inches."

"Sorry. Why do you want to kill him now?" He asks.

"I'm fucking done with this shit. Who knows when it's going to end? Some of these guys have been out here for fucking years. Look at that dude, he looks like he's sucking on half a plum, but he's not. It's just that all of his teeth are shot out."

"So why kill General Jackson?"

"To speed this shit up and end this war. If he dies, it's just Lee—and that isn't going to be enough. Look, this place we're going tomorrow—Chancellorsville—we're going to be outnumbered again by almost three to one," I say in a hushed tone.

"How do you know?"

"This girl who was blowing me the other night in my tent told me—

"How do you keep getting blowjobs inside your tent over and over—

"There's no time for that awesome story Daniel! What's important is that we cap off Stonewall and make it look like friendly fire. The North will roll through after that and we can leave. Go back west."

Daniel shakes his head. "I don't know if I can leave without my wife."

I puff up with pride as I pull the nude portrait of Louretta out of my pants and unroll it for Daniel. "If your mom could see you right now, she'd say—why are you staring at my bush?" I say as I rub the portrait all over his face.

"Jesus Dad! Stop," Daniel says embarrassed.

"It's your mother's bush, show some fucking respect. Yes, you can bring your wife if you want. Now if it were me personally, you got your father back as your wingman, I wouldn't waste that opportunity to make a strong poon run."

"I know Dad, but she's special. Just like Mom was," he says pointing to the bush portrait.

I slap his knee and fire up a heater, acknowledging her bush again. "We'll let this battle go down, kill Stonewall, and take off to get your wife as the Union starts to take control. Cool?"

"Fine. I'm in," Daniel says as he takes a drag off my smoke.

A man holding a large drum from the makeshift band around the campfire, taps his sticks off the rim. "Would you care to join us Mr. Street James?"

"Not tonight boys. We got an early battle and all," I say.

Daniel leans over. "Yeah that's smart. We should get back to our tents—

"Alright, maybe I can do one more!" I say as I pull out a harmonica and expertly begin to play *Oh Susanna* a whole half note lower, just because I can.

As I reach the one hour and thirty-eight-minute mark, I look around at these faces, knowing this is probably the end for them. They'll all more than likely be killed, so I decide to give them this one last gift of brilliance. I see Stonewall Jackson grooving along, taking a pull from a stogie. I'll never forget the look on that smug son of a bitch's face when he had that black midget pull a straight razor on me. I can still smell his dank pubes like it happened five minutes ago.

That kind of smell lives with a man his whole life. If someone's taint comes that close to your nostrils, it's burned in there forever. If I get coffee, that first inhale before I take a sip is still a brief smell of taint, then the actual coffee scent. It's also one of those smells that you think you smell everywhere, but you actually don't. It's very piquant. I don't know where I was when Neil Armstrong landed on the moon, but goddamnit if I don't smell Stonewall Jackson's scrotum coaster every day.

After I finish the performance, I throw the harmonica into the fire, and curtsy to General Jackson. The crowd goes crazy, so I pull out my dick. Don't even bother questioning it, I'm not going to apologize for being an emotional performer. With the soldiers now at fever pitch, I piss out the entire campfire, extinguishing the flames with the same equivalent of a fire hose at max level during a four-alarmer. I shake twice, and retuck, before bowing to my audience.

"Let's get some sleep boys! Big day of the same exact shit you've been doing for years now with little to no result," I say with a half-ass salute.

I walk back to the tent and see Daniel pulling his hat over his eyes, getting ready for bed. Kneeling down, I pat his chest, assuring him everything will be alright—with the prostitute that is rolling by later. It's important that he knows I have one coming over.

"Daniel, you mind taking off your belt so she can choke me, or vice versa? I'm getting real tired of the standard beej," I casually tell him.

"What's wrong with your belt?" He asks annoyed.

"I've got this weird amputee fetish with myself. I use my own belt and tie it around my leg as hard as I can like a tourniquet, until there's no feeling in it. Somehow it makes me feel mortal."

"Yeah, fine. Here. I just want to get some sleep," he says as he takes off his belt and hands it to me.

"You don't have half a scissor lying around that I could stab myself with as I climax—

Daniel turns over facing his side of the tent. "Goodnight Dad!"

The next morning, I arise bright and early, feeling a certain sense of calm before the storm. Probably because when I looked down, the prostitute from the night before was still sleeping with my penis buried in her mouth. I push her gently off of me and walk outside the tent, seeing soldiers now stirring about making breakfast. This is the day I end this bullshit.

I walk over to a group of younger soldiers who are enjoying a cup of coffee and promptly drink it, because who the fuck cares. One of them is reading a local paper, so I rip it out of his hands on the way to the shitter. These aren't K-cups, Holmes. These are mashed up beans running straight through my intestines, so I have about two minutes before an Ecuador mudslide hits.

Unfolding the paper as I sit down in the outhouse, I see a picture of Harriet Tubman with eight other slaves on the front page. The caption reads: "**Woman Wanted For Running Underground Railroad For Slaves.**" Son of a bitch. There's no toilet paper in here. I'm also super angry about the slave thing. Fuck it. I get up and pull my pants up without wiping. This is the last time I'm wearing this goddamn uniform anyway, might as well mudslide it.

I kick open the outhouse door and throw the newspaper into the fire in front of the dude I took it from. As I head over to my tent, I see the prostitute's leg sticking out, so I assume she's giving Daniel a freebie, hoping for a loose change tip afterward. I'm not going to disturb him. A hand squeezes the back of my arm tightly. I turn and jerk my pistol. It's Stonewall, sipping a tin cup of coffee. He smiles at me.

"You ready for battle today? This is going to be a big one. It's going to take everything in you. I want you close to me today out there," he says.

"Oh, I'll be close. I promise," I say through a thinly veiled smile.

"Good! Looking forward to a resounding victory!"

"Uh-huh. How's that joe?" I ask, knowing the fucking answer.

"It's running through me like Pamplona? You gone yet? I could use a dump brother[*] on this one."

"No, I beefed one out already. I'll see you out there," I say with a wink.

He pats me on the shoulder and walks hurriedly toward the outhouse. I didn't bother to tell him that it was out of toilet paper. I'd like his last day on earth to be as shitty as mine.

On my walk back, I see the prostitute walking out of the tent with lipstick smeared all over her face like that homemade clown video of Anna Nicole Smith right before she died. The prosty winks at me and throws in a beaver dip before walking out into town. Daniel pops out right after her, putting his belt back through the loops. I look at him sternly.

"I'M GOING TO TELL YOUR FUCKING WIFE WHAT YOU DID YOU SON OF A BITCH!" I say as I get into his face.

He looks mortified. "What? Please don't do that. She would—

---

[*] A dump brother is someone who sits in the outhouse next to you that you chat with and share your excrement experience. It's very spiritual.

109

I can barely contain my laughter. "I'm just fisting your b-hole. You think I give a fuck? Come on my dude! Let's go kill a General!"

"Okay. Jesus. That was aggressive. How do you plan on doing this by the way?" He asks looking over his shoulder making sure no one is around.

"Actually, he grabbed me and asked me to be his dump brother, then told me he wanted me to stay close to him today on the battlefield. You ride with me, and when the time is right and no one is around, we drop that motherfucker. Cool?"

"Sounds good," he says.

"Aces. I'm going to grab my steed. Also, one more thing, that girl who re-headed you after me this morning threw in a beaver dip after she walked out of the tent. Chew on that thought the rest of the day," I say as I fire an invisible six shooter at him.

He shakes his head. "I didn't need to know that."

"That's exactly why I said it," I say with a laugh.

We saddle up and ride into Chancellorsville, surveying the battlefield right behind General Jackson. Holy shit. When I say there is a fuck ton of Union soldiers on the other side, I mean they are as far as the eye can see. We rolled up with a third of their soldiers, maybe close to half if I'm being generous. Whatever our final head count was, it rhymed with "not-e-fucking-nough."

The one thing I'll say about the Confederate soldiers is this; these are tough motherfuckers who didn't give a shit. When you grow up in the back woods shooting weird fucking animals and skinning them to wear or eat since age five, it really develops a good healthy dose of that "fuck you" spirit—because let's be real—if you can kill shit on your own and you don't give a fuck where you live, who's going to stop you from doing anything in this life? Certainly not these pussies from the North. At the end of the day though, numbers are numbers. No matter how badass you are, it's tough to take out this many bastards over and over again and continuously pull out wins but—

Guess who had two thumbs, no taint hair, and didn't give a shit? Stonewall Jackson. I sat on my steed and observed him on his horse as he looked out at the battlefield through binoculars. The motherfucker was motionless. It was just another day at the J-O-B for this dude.

"Let's skip the drummer boy bullshit and start firing the cannons. I want to get on with this shit," Jackson said to his lieutenant.

The lieutenant nodded and rode off back to the rest of the soldiers with the instructions. General Jackson clicked his horse back over to mine and handed me his binoculars. I looked at him surprised.

"Twelve o'clock. Have a look," he said with a smile.

I lift the binoculars up to my face and aim them at my twelve o'clock. "You mean those two little kids walking out—

BOOM!!!

"Fuck!" I yell out as I see a huge cannonball blow up the two drummer boys from the Union.

Stonewall Jackson laughs. "When do you ever get to see shit like this? Am I right?"

"I have to admit, it was the last thing I was expecting to see today," I say as I laugh with him. "That was fucking great."

"Alright, after the first wave of our soldiers run in and get killed, you lead the second wave and fuck shit up," he said matter of factly.

"Aren't you coming?" I ask curiously.

"No, General Lee is leading another group of soldiers around the bend up north. He wants to use the element of surprise by splitting us into two units to try and tackle these motherfuckers. There's more Union soldiers than this you know? Probably double the amount of the men you see before you," he says motioning at the Union soldiers who are still reeling from the blast.

"*Twice* the soldiers of these?" I ask with surprise.

"Yeah. It's like they have every single Yankee ever born entering this war. I'll be riding back after darkness to catch up

112

with the proceedings here," he says as he slaps me on the shoulder.

I glance over at Daniel, then back to Stonewall. "I'll see you tonight."

"Just follow the stink. There was no fucking toilet paper in the crapper this morning, so I'm riding dirty the rest of the day. Who does shit like that? Leave a note or something, you know?" Jackson asks, shaking his head in disgust.

Stonewall tips his cap angrily and rides off down a trail into the woods. He seemed more concerned about the stink rather than the fucking all out war that was now taking place below us on the battlefield. Even though I was going to kill him, I fucking respected the shit out of him. Dude was an absolute fucking gangster through and through. When people asked me about him over the years, I've always said that dude was about that life. It was no bullshit.

After the usual first shots fired, soldiers from both sides charging at each other on foot, then people stabbing each other with bayonets—Daniel and I rode in. Old school. Just like the Wild West days, popping people off with six shooters. Nobody was taking me off my goddamn steed, especially during battle.

Daniel lived up to the hype too. He really is a close second behind me as far as his shot goes. Together, we were a deadly combo picking off Union soldiers with precision. As much as we didn't care about the war, fact of the matter is, you're wearing the other uniform—you kill them or they kill you. Simple as that. The thrill of the kill is still there at least.

After a few hours, and what seemed to be a surprising victory considering the number of soldiers we were against, Daniel and I head back toward the trail where Stonewall had left us. I rip off some water canteens from the necks of some dead Union soldiers and hydrate my steed. Initially, he turns up his nose at me, motioning his snout toward my pants.

"No TP friend. Sorry you got stained. I'll make it up to you," I said.

My horse nodded back at me unimpressed. He's heard it a thousand times. I give him half of my loaf of bread as Daniel ties up his steed as well.

"What's the play now, Dad?"

I eye a nice spot on the ridgeline to get off a clean shot. "There," I say as I point to a gap between two trees about thirty yards uphill.

Daniel eyes it. "That's a little too far for pistols," he says.

"Yeah, we're going to have to go with the rifles," I say as I lick my finger and hold it up to check the wind.

"We're only going to get one shot a piece with those fucking things before someone comes looking. They'll take forever to reload," he says.

"I smile at him with that classic Saint James Street James James devilish grin. Then you better not miss," I say.

He shakes his head. "Again, Dad, you don't have to describe yourself as you're talking to me."

"Was I doing that again? Goddamnit I'm awesome. Let's face it, if there's someone who deserves to narrate himself, it's me. Grab some food and meet me up on the hill," I say as I begin walking up.

As day turned into night, it started getting pretty fucking late. Thoughts of apprehension started racing through my mind. What if they were defeated? What if he was killed with Lee in the other battle? I wonder what time that whorehouse in town was open until? So many questions were pondered.

Finally, just after midnight, I hear a horse riding up over the hill, followed by that unmistakable stink. Like I said, I was down wind, so I could smell him. It was a good thing too, because it was so late, it was really fucking hard to see. In essence, that mud-butt smell really helped. I tap Daniel on the shoulder and hold up my index finger as he trains his rifle on Stonewall riding in.

"On my call," I whisper to him.

"Yup," he says without a hint of nerves. This little motherfucker has grown into in hardened killer.

"3...2...1... Fire," I say.

BLAM!

We both fire simultaneously hitting Stonewall with bullets in the chest and arm. Obviously, I hit him in the chest, because I'm still best shot there is. It appears as if Daniel's shot shattered his fucking arm. Stonewall's horse takes off into the night, spooked as shit. I motion for Daniel to pack it up quietly and get out of here, people will be looking for where the gunfire came from shortly. Daniel and I were long gone before anyone got there.

Later on we heard that his aides rode in a few moments later and found him. They tried to save him, but apparently Daniel's shot that shattered his arm forced it to be amputated, and he died from pneumonia from the surgery a few days later. Isn't that some bullshit? I hit that motherfucker square in the chest, but an arm shot kills him? Fuck me between the folds of my balloon knot. The Confederate military listed his death as "friendly fire", but we sure the fuck weren't friends. Not after the gooch blade he pulled on me. *Via con dios.*

This is why there were so many fucked up injuries in the Civil War, the bullets weren't deadly enough, and you usually had to fucking stab somebody a gajillion times to get the job done. Typically, people ended up dying because they didn't have penicillin or some shit like that. If you were getting an arm or leg amputated, forget it. They took a fucking table saw out and told you to bite down on the shitty bullet that *didn't* kill you. What a cruel way to die. I'm kidding. I didn't fucking care. If he was rad enough, he'd still be alive.

As Daniel and I trucked it through the forest back to his house to grab his wife that night, we ran right into General Lee and the other unit setting up camp for the night. Son of a bitch. Lee and a bunch of the higher ups were sitting around a fire sipping whiskey out of tin cups. As our horses approached, he looked up, surprised to see me.

"What are you doing here Mr. Street James?" Lee asked, slightly buzzed.

I had to think quick. "Uh, we killed all those other dudes, so we were like—let's go check out the sights while we're here. My son is an avid bird watcher."

General Lee sits up in shock. "Wait a minute, you guys won on that side?"

"Yeah, man. They're all dead. I mean, there's a few that were still groaning and shit, but they'll obviously die in a few days," I say nonchalantly.

"We were outnumbered by almost three to one over there! Hot damn! I knew splitting the men up and fighting from the north would do it! Is Stonewall partying or what?" Lee asks with exuberation.

"You know, we didn't see him. It's super dark, and like my Dad says, I'm an *avid bird watcher*, so I wanted to see the night owls. Look, there's one right over there," Daniel says as he motions to a tree.

Blam!

Daniel shoots the fucking owl right off the tree branch and it falls over dead on the ground—or at least it *will probably be dead in a few days*. Lee looks at him impressed. He stands up and brings over the bottle of whiskey.

"You two are fucking crazy! I love it!" he says as he hands me the bottle of whiskey. "I want you guys with me from now on. You two are never leaving my side, you understand?"

"Yup," I say about as unenthusiastically as one can.

He looks at his aides and says, "We're going to win this goddamn war after all boys!"

Holy Christ. I have to keep going with these assholes? I'm going to have to kill this motherfucker too.

Chapter 7

PEYOTE BUTTONS AND TENT SEX

June 30, 1863
Gettysburg, Pennsylvania

After the victory at Chancellorsville, General Lee marched us up to Pennsylvania in June, never once leaving my side with his aides. I thought about capping this fucking guy every last goddamn second of every single day, but we were surrounded 24/7 by a shit ton of people. The Stonewall sitch was ideal. It was dark, there was no one around, and we were in the middle of the fucking woods. A move against Lee here would have cost me my life. This motherfucker was ruthless too.

Robert E. Lee rolled through towns like he was Floyd Mayweather. There was always an entourage of people, zero fucks given. Instead of throwing out money, he was dishing out bullets. I guess when you win as many battles as he did constantly being outnumbered, your dick grows a few more inches and you don't care. Needless to say, Daniel and I were fucking miserable.

With the Confederates coming to town, and me under lock and key with General Lee, I sent Daniel to get the word out to Tubman to get the fuck out of here. What if Lee was able to pull off this state as well? I wasn't going to risk it and my sweet Nubian princess needed to be warned. Shit, I still can't even believe we got this far up North.

When Daniel came back a few hours later, he told me she was grateful. She had him give me a note as well. When I open it, there was only one sentence on it; *You owe me a window motherfucker. ~Tubbs.* Damn. She's fucking hilarious. Championship move.

With camp set up, and another battle looming tomorrow in Gettysburg, I prepare myself the only way I know how; by getting some prosties. General Lee said if I needed anything to just send a couple privates into town and they would take care of it. Obviously, I took full advantage of this.

"You there," I say motioning to two young men milling around a tent. "Come over here, I need some shit from town."

The two privates walk over and stand at attention. "Yes sir," one of them says. Upon closer examination they look like teenagers.

"Jesus. How old are you guys?" I ask.

"I just turned sixteen and my brother just turned fifteen, sir," he replies in a thick southern accent.

"You guys Irish twins?"

They look at me confused. "No sir, we're from Georgia," the other one says.

"It's a joke that has already sailed past your head like the fucking *Santa Maria*. Anyway, I need something from town."

"Of course. What is it sir?" The brother asks.

"Something for my dick. It's sensitive," I say in a serious tone.

"I'm sorry sir, your dick is sensitive?" The other brother asks, trying to understand.

"No man. The matter is sensitive, I need prostitutes for my dick. You know, whores? Women of the night. Poon candy. Taco vendors. Brothel guts. Trollups. Some female residents from Big Bone Lick State Park. Do you understand?"

They stare at me with their mouths agape, before one of them finally speaks. "Sir, we ain't never been to no whorehouses before. We're too young."

"Nonsense. You're fighting a fucking war, you're old enough to die, so therefore you're old enough to fuck if you want. I took my son when he was your age. Look, here's what I want you to do. I'm going to give you twenty dollars, you bring me back four whores. One of them must be Indian. You understand me?"

"Yes sir, but—

"I don't care about their butts, huge tits is my game. Also, you can take the extra money and bang whoever you want. Do not, I repeat, DO NOT fuck any of the girls you're bringing back to me. I'll fucking know, so don't even try it."

"Um, okay," the brothers say in unison as I hand them twenty dollars.

"Don't fuck me on that Indian chick. I need an Indian in the mix tonight. I'll be in my tent over there, so that's where they are to be delivered," I say as I motion to my tent.

As they walk away, I head over to Daniel who is carving something out of a piece of tree with a buck knife. I sit down next to him on a log and light up a cig. I'd offer him one, but I only have thirty left.

"What are you carving son?" I ask.

"It's going to be a compass so I—

"Rhetorical. You know I don't care about arts and crafts bullshit. No one does," I say as I inhale a monster drag.

General Lee walks over to us. He looks down at Daniel's homemade compass with disdain. "What's that fag shit?"

"It's a compass—

"I don't fucking care. You guys ready for battle tomorrow? This is going to be a nasty one," Lee says.

"Yeah man, we're good. Going to retire early tonight, so I'm all rested and what-the-fuck-not," I say.

"That's what I like to hear! See you out there!" The General exclaims as he and his minions walk away.

Daniel looks at me oddly. "You? Retiring early to rest up?"

"Fuck no, man. I got some privates to track me down some prosties so I can get loose. There was none on this fucking ride up here, and daddy needs his fix. How many times have you heard me say this shit at this point?"

"That's more like it," he says shaking his head.

"Speaking of which, if you see a sock hanging on the outside of the tent, don't even fucking bother coming in. I got four on the way, so it's going to be a tight squeeze tent-wise. You might need to take your sleeping bag outside tonight."

"I know the drill," he says.

"I bet it's going to be a nice night under the stars according to your compass," I say pointing down at the carved wood.

"A compass doesn't measure the solar system it's for—

"I'm done trying to pretend to care," I say as I walk off back to the tent.

As soon as I'm inside, I take Daniel's sleeping bag and immediately chuck it out of the tent and pin a sock to the outside. To be extra cautious, I put up a wooden sign that I had painted earlier that read "**DON'T FUCKING COME IN**" in giant red letters. I really needed these prosties tonight. There's some things that are sacred in this world, and prostitution is obviously one of them. I *really* hope I drove this point home from the last book all the way through this one so far, because prostitution is something I hold near and very dear to my heart.

Around 10pm that night, I hear the two younger soldiers giggling as they deliver the whores after dark. They totally used the extra cash to fuck, which makes me smile. I've never been a big "giver" to charities, helping people in need, or extending a hand to *any* people going through a real crisis—but I have doled out a few sheckles here and there for some dudes to get their fuck on. Truthfully, that probably meant more to them than any homeless guy I could have ever fed—so let's celebrate me— instead of trying to tear me down.

The whores these guys brought back were legit. These chicks had come with their *A game*. What I particularly nice is that they weren't trashy, instead they had a plain natural beauty to them. Years later, fashion experts would call this look

"Midwestern". They have some meat on them, but they aren't fat. Their features are curvy and inviting like an over-sized fleece on a chilly winter afternoon. You could tell they'd stay and eat with you afterward, because they brought a shit ton of food.

Now the Indian girl, she was different. She was a halfer, not full blood. A half-blooded Indian was crazy enough to have a good time, but you wouldn't have to worry about her trying to bury an Arrowhead into your neck after you were done fucking. Instead of food, she pulled out a folded piece of cloth from a pocket in her dress, which contained a handful of peyote buttons. *Whoopsie ding-dong.* Time to fucking party.

She smiles at me and holds up a button.

"This is from the Chihuahuan Desert," she says.

"I know it well. These buttons are from the cactus that can be found in areas of Texas and Mexico, which is common among scrub where there is limestone settlement," I say as I take her gift and put it in my mouth.

She seems genuinely taken back by that. "That's incredible. How do you know that?"

I smile sweetly at her. "I've taken copious amounts of drugs in my day. By you even seeming the least bit surprised undermines me for who I am as a man. Now please disrobe and disperse the drugs evenly amongst the whores."

125

She looks down and spots a map lying on the ground next to my sleeping bag. "What's the map for?"

I blush and turn away. "Oh that? That tells me where the fuck I'm going."

She takes off her dress and begins to slowly dance in place above the map, before leaning down to pick it up. Holding it loosely in the air, she begins to wave it back and forth very sensually. She snaps her fingers, which creates a small flame from the lower corner of the map. It ignites pretty quickly, burning in mid-air.

"Tonight, we don't need a map. I'll be your guide," she says before sauntering over to kiss me.

That map going up in flames has me shook. How could I be tripping balls this fucking quickly? Fucking Indians man. This shit was so intense. The other women start taking off their clothes, before slowly laying me down on the ground of the tent. When they pull my boots off, it's as if they are pulling my legs clean off my body. There is a warm sensation coursing through me, and my boner was on that max level where you feel as if you're going to run out of skin.

The Indian began to ride me as the others made out with each other. One of the girls took what appears to be a pine tree branch and begins slapping another girl's tits with it. I don't know what the fuck is going on. I close my eyes for a second and when I open them, the Indian girl's face has turned into a wolf. The wild thing was, I welcomed it. As I look around at the other three, their faces have morphed into oxen. All of them still have normal human bodies, but animal faces. It is the fucking greatest thing ever.

I know what you're thinking, "Did you *want* to fuck animals Saint James Street James?" No. That was never a bucket list item, but in this moment it felt right. The screams that were coming out of their mouths as the sex heightened were primal. I'm talking deep guttural groans from within, like spirits screaming from underneath the ground.

The strange thing about tripping on peyote is you're not often just receiving visual hallucinations; auditory hallucinations are common as well. Most of the sounds I am hearing are violent, piercing screams that are either pleasure or pain. I hear fireworks going off. Flesh being ripped open and I wasn't even sure if it was mine. At one point a live chicken was running through the tent with one leg missing. I am fucking blasted out of my skull right now.

What I did know, is that I don't have a care in the world. I let the Indian girl be my guide. When she got off, I watch her walk across the tent and jump into a cupboard. Was that where she came from in the first place? Is any of this real? How tall am I? There was so many questions that I just couldn't answer.

One by one each girl begins to mount me, and the sex feels comfortable and familiar. There was no agenda—probably because they were all prepaid—and it wasn't going to be a "hang on, I forgot my my wallet at my buddy's house and never come back" type of night. This felt different. Special. I felt like the stream and they felt like the salmon that needed to swim through. Again, I really can't emphasize how high I am at this point. I never say shit like this, but I totally thought it at the time.

I'm not even sure how long this lasted, or who I was anymore. Also, was the Indian still in the cupboard? Who fucking knows. After a few hours it seemed like time and space collided. I could sure use Daniel's compass now, or whatever the fuck you use that bullshit thing for, because I was gone.

The following morning, I awake to the sounds of concerned voices and footsteps outside my tent. War is fucking bullshit dude. Nobody can keep it the fuck down and respect the fact that a tent is a goddamn home, there's no reason to be a dick about it by talking right outside of it. And why is everything so fucking "urgent" all the time? Get the fuck over it.

I try to get up, but obviously I'm having a real tough time. Mostly because all four women are sleeping on top of me. I push them off, and then punch myself in the face. I've got a *Weekend At Bernie's* type hangover where I literally have to hold my fucking eyelids open to try and act alive. One man's high pitched,

Peter Brady-ish voice stands out from the rest, and holy shit I'm going to kill myself if he says another fucking word—

"My God. Look at all this carnage. The shear size and scope of it is far greater than I expected", the man says in his pitchy voice directly outside my tent now.

I'm assuming the way the sun is hitting the tent, he's describing my cock from the outside, which probably looks like the front end of the *Titanic* sticking up from out of the water after it hit the iceberg. It's great that he respects my brilliance, but the morning after a peyote orgy is a no go for me until at least 5pm. Not wanting to hear another word exit his skull cave, I hastily get up and walk out of the tent. Ten Union soldiers draw their rifles as they stare at me in shock. Probably because I'm butt ass naked, and half erect. I'm not even wearing a sock, bro. I'm talking clean nude, wearing nothing but my beard.

I hold my hands up in front of my face, because the sun is literally raping my eyes out right now. It's hard to make out who they are or who was talking. I squint at the biggest one and yell in the direction of the man out in front.

"You want to use your inside voice chief? Shit was popping off last night, and this soldier hasn't stopped saluting the four broads in my tent all night", I say as I point at my dick.

The man out in front stares at me strangely before replying, "Are you a Confederate soldier or a Union soldier—

"Honestly, every time you speak I want to take a dull butter knife and slice my fucking ears off. Can you make your balls drop and speak to me like a man?"

"Watch your mouth son. You're speaking to the President of the United States, Abraham Lincoln. If you do not contain your tongue, I will be forced to kill you," one of Union soldiers says.

Well fuck. This is it. I'm fucking done for I thought. Instead of running like a bitch, I pull out a solemn cigarette and a pack of matches that I have taped behind my scrotum in case of an emergency, and fire up a morning heater to try and regain my senses. I exhale loudly and adjust my eyes to the sunlight.

Upon further review, it really is Abraham Lincoln. Motherfucker. I know what you're thinking, "Dude, you're the only one who's still alive on this earth that has gotten to meet him in person, what was he like?" Keeping it one hundred, he was *exactly like Daniel Day-Lewis in that fucking movie.* I'm blanking on the name of it, but Google it. I don't know if Speilberg gave DDL access to the *Back To The Future* Delorean, or if he is actually a fucking time traveler—but that son of a bitch was *him.*

"Do you even know where you are son? Thousands are dead, man. This is the worst battle this country has ever seen!" one of his General's says.

I rub my eyes. "That battle already happened? It wasn't supposed to start until this morning?"

The Union General looks at me enraged. "Which morning was that?"

"July 1st that shit was supposed to go down," I say as I take a drag.

"Son, today is July 5th. Hold on, do you mean to tell me you slept through the entire Battle of Gettysburg for the last four days?" Abraham Lincoln asks in disbelief.

"Well, I wasn't exactly sleeping," I say as I open the tent revealing all four nude women.

"Jesus Christ. You had an orgy throughout this entire event?" His General asks exasperated.

This dude looked like he was about to have a fucking melt down. I couldn't help but chuckle.

"Fucking peyote man. What are you going to do, am I right? You really lose track of time," I say motioning to an invisible watch I'm not wearing.

With my eyes now somewhat adjusted to the sunlight, I look around the battlefield and see bodies piled on top of other bodies. It stretches as far as the eye can see. Both Union and Confederate soldiers are strewn out everywhere. Men are missing limbs, some are in shallow graves, it's pretty gruesome.

Glad I fucked through all that shit and missed it. I take a long inhale off my smoke and scratch my head.

"Well that's war I guess. One minute you're alive and fucking, the next minute—DANIEL!!!!"

About ten yards from the tent I see Daniel lying face up, his body once again riddled with bullets. I run over and violently try to shake him awake. Nothing. I start performing chest compressions, before switching my position, realizing my cock was in his face.

Now in the proper position, I begin trying to revive him. It's no use. He's dead. I stand up and turn my anger toward the Union soldiers.

"Did you fucking do this shit Abe? I swear to God I will kill you *then* rape you!" I scream, fury running through every fabric of my being.

The Union soldiers cock their guns. "Stand down! Stand down!" they demand.

The Union General looks at me curiously, before suddenly blurting out, "You're Saint James Street James! You're wanted for killing hundreds of Marshals!"

He reaches into his pocket and unfolds my all nude Wanted poster, which is completely ironic right now. The rest of the soldiers peek over at the poster and confirm my identity. A couple of them nod in amazement at how accurate the drawing is. I told you it was to scale.

Realizing this is the end of the road, I'm going out like a fucking boss. I go charging straight for Lincoln. The other soldiers immediately rush in and try and tackle me to the ground to no avail. I've got too much adrenaline rushing through me, and since I'm not wearing clothing, they have nothing to grasp on to.

Abraham Lincoln holds up his hand. "Let him go boys. I've lost a son. If he wants to fight, let's fight like men. One on one."

I nod, impressed. "No shit. Abraham Lincoln wants to knuckle the fuck up, huh? Let's do work kid", I say as I crack my neck back and forth like Tom Hardy in *Warrior*.

"Let'em fly", Abe says as he takes off his long black coat and circles me. "Do you want to put some clothes on first?"

"Not a goddamn prayer", I say as I lick the palm of my right hand and smack my own dick downward in a show of dominance. I wanted him to know that I was seriously going to fuck him up. What kind of man smacks his own dong? A hard ass motherfucker like me, that's who. And yeah, I fought Abraham Lincoln buck naked. Go ahead and let that sugar cube dissolve in your tea while this whole shit sinks in.

I ball up my fists and walk over to this tall drink of shit, landing a vicious right hook to the side of his dome. He retreats backward. I smile as his head snaps back, thinking this is going to be an easy fight. In my mind right now, I'm thinking this is going to be some Kimbo Slice showing up in a Miami neighborhood YouTube type fight, you know? *Wrong.*

The honest one spits out some blood and smiles back at me, before ripping off a sick one two combo knocking me off my feet. This son of a bitch has a reach like no other. At this point, I know I'm in for an all out street brawl. I grab two fingers full of mud and smear them underneath my eyes, before standing back up. It's time to get tribal on this motherfucker.

I deliver a roundhouse kick toward his face, which he expertly dodges, before bending down and sweeping my leg. I hit the mud again hard as I fall on my back. I do a sweet *kip up* and thrust myself back to my feet. Enough of the dumb shit. I square up and feint a jab then land a body blow directly to his solar plexus. He doubles over from the pain and I send him to the ground with a violent knee to the face. Blood is now pouring from this ugly motherfucker's mug.

He takes a moment to reorient himself, while he snaps his broken nose back into place. I smirk at him as his men decide whether they should intervene or not.

"I wouldn't worry about fixing the handle, that umbrella was already busted", I say to him, pointing at his face.

He wipes blood from his nostrils and stares at me. "You think I'm ugly?"

"If I'm being *honest*, you're the worst looking dude I've ever seen. It was probably a smart choice to throw a little spinach around that potato," I say motioning to his chin strap beard.

This enrages him. He charges at me like a bull who just got his dick chopped off and tackles me hard to the ground. As each of us grapple for leverage, he head butts me. My noggin whips back, and he begins unleashing a flurry of quick punches to my face. I manage to leg wrap him and flip him backwards. Now it is me who is on top of him dropping bombs to his head.

My raw natural power is too much for what little old man strength he has left. Dude was a fucking lawyer; it wasn't like I was fighting George fucking Washington for Christ sakes. I begin pummeling him into the ground, over and over again.

"This is for Daniel!" I scream.

With his face quickly becoming a bloody mess, one of his Union soldiers runs over and bashes me in the head with the butt of his rifle. I fly backwards off of Lincoln into the mud. My forehead is split open like Hulk Hogan's in almost every *WrestleMania* ever. The other soldiers quickly form a circle around me and cock their rifles as I laugh maniacally.

"You got any last words?" One of them asks.

"Yeah. Does my dick make me look fat?" I say as I reach down and grab it one last time. I smell the air, wanting to catch one last whiff of that sex smell wafting from my tent.

"I'm going to blow it straight up your asshole," the Union soldier says with a grin.

Just as the men are about to squeeze their triggers, Lincoln stands up and shouts, "Don't shoot him. It was a fair fight that I engaged with him."

"What? You can't be serious sir? This man is wanted for multiple murders," the soldier says shocked.

The men stand down and Lincoln pushes through the circle, extending his hand down to me. I grab it out of respect and he lifts me up. Fucking Lincoln man. He really was a fair and just dude. Once I'm to my feet, I look down at myself and see that I'm caked in more mud than my second night at Woodstock and blood is still streaming down my face. Lincoln looks me square in the eye and nods his head, acknowledging my fighting prowess.

"Why don't we get cleaned up and you tell me about your boy?" He asks.

"Is 'tell me about your boy' code for me blowing you? Because if so, I'm not cool with that."

Lincoln cocks his head back and laughs like an old woman missing her shoes. "No, but that's a good one. Let's just share a whiskey and a bath like men", he says slapping me on the back.

"That still sounds kind of gay, but I'll give it a go. Just let me grab my left hook—

I turn and knock out the soldier that smashed my skull in with his rifle. He falls backwards, laid out like a snow angel in the mud. Lincoln laughs. The other soldiers stare at me in anger, but there's nothing they could do, I was about to go take a bath with the president.

"Gentlemen, please put the man's son in a nice coffin and promptly take him to my cabin", Lincoln says over his shoulder as we walk off the battlefield.

I whistle for my steed and ride along side Lincoln into town. As we hit a nice stride, a group of white wingless doves fly in front of us at top speed, causing me to pull back on the reigns of my horse. That's when I realize I'm still dipping in and out of hallucinations, before eventually just chalking it up to the peyote. Turns out there were definitely no birds at all, but the Battle of Gettysburg was a weird four days for me.

Chapter 8

WAILWOADS ARE WHEEL

Abraham Lincoln and I sit in two adjacent tubs about three feet a part, smoking cigars, drinking whiskey, and sharing a cock soak. The bleeding has subsided on his face, and I have some slight swelling around my left eye. Despite our differences, it's nice when two dudes who just kicked the shit out of one another can come together and share a bath.

"Tell me about yourself," Lincoln asks.

"Well, I'm 6'3", 215, and obviously I'm throwing around nine flaccid from the waist down—

"No, no, no. Tell me something about your life. Where you came from, who you really are. Are you married?"

"I'm from California originally, and yes, I *was* married. A house fire took my wife and my first seven children. The eighth one just died out there today, or one of the last four days. I'll never really have the answer to that because of the peyote," I say as I take a sip of my whiskey.

"I'm sorry to hear that. Do you know how the fire started?" He asks.

"US Marshals came out at the behest of Former-President Van Buren. They were unhappy with my business dealings, so they burned my house down and killed my family."

Abraham shakes his head, "Fucking eight."

"I'm sorry, what?" I ask.

"Us presidents call each other by number, I'm sixteen, he was fucking eight."

"Gotcha," I say with a smile.

"One of the founders of the Democratic party. Dude was a real asshole. He passed away last year in Kinderhook, New York. Some of my representatives asked me to go, which I did hastily at the last minute. I wasn't happy about it. At the end of the night, I pissed on his grave," he says taking a puff off his cigar.

I can't help but laugh. "No shit? You hated him that much?"

"Yeah, I did. You have no idea how hard the Democrats fought to try and stop me from abolishing slavery. I have a feeling they're going to be spending the rest of their lives trying to make up for it one day," he says wistfully as he takes another puff on his cigar.

"Their great-great grand kids will probably even be protesting too. Fucking dipshits," I say.

He turns and looks at me surprised. "You're not against slavery?"

"Nope. Matter a fact, I got down with a black chick about a year ago, and it was majestic."

"So why are you fighting for the Confederates?" He asks puzzled.

"No where else to go. Marshals wanted me dead, and the Rebels—well they didn't give a shit that I was an outlaw. I came out East looking for my last remaining son, and I ended up in the middle of this shit. Truthfully, I just want to go back to California," I say as I drink the rest of my whiskey and slide his glass over to me when he's not looking over.

"The Wild West," he says looking skyward as if he's lost in thought. "I've never been to California. How is it?" He asks, genuinely interested.

"Weather is nice. People are fucking weird. Shit definitely gets wild. You gotta be real handy with your steel, if you know what I mean," I say pointing down at my pistols on the floor.

"I've always wanted to dip my dick in the Pacific. Hopefully with the legislation I passed last year, I'll be able to see it soon," he says wistfully.

"What legislation is that?" I ask.

"I signed a bill for the first transcontinental railroad. It's going to go all the way from the Atlantic to the Pacific. When it's completed, I'm going to take the first train out there to celebrate it in San Francisco."

"Fun town. Their bath houses are unmatched. Bring your fishnets," I say as I now drink his whiskey.

"You know, I heard the fishing is good there."

"Yeah, if *fishing* means fucking other dudes. Lot of gays there," I say with a laugh. "I'm talking about fishnet stockings, holmes."

He seems taken back. "Oh. Jesus."

"Yeah, I've spent some time in San Fran. They got great laborers though. The Chinese work really cheap and efficient."

"Sounds like you know California pretty well," he says impressed.

"I do. I also spent about six years in China. Those dudes are dying to come here and work. They'd do it all the live long day. I had over a hundred of them working for me on my ranch. Those fuckers were relentless," I say as I ash my stogie in my tub.

"You know, I could use a man to oversee it. Someone who has spent some time there and is good with those type of laborers. It could be a decent job and a way for you to start over since you lost your entire family," he says with a cocked eyebrow.

I look at him intrigued. "Me? You want me to be in charge of the first transcontinental railroad?"

"Sure. I heard they've had some rough times getting going with Indians and what-not. A lot of robberies. I could use someone a little rough around the edges to help complete it," he says motioning toward his beat up face.

I chuckle to myself and finish his whiskey. "Me working for the government? That's a fucking fat man's laugh. You'd have to pardon me though. I can't deal with these Marshals hounding me."

"I can do that. After this victory in Gettysburg, the war is almost over. Now we just need to unite the country and expand west. Start improving commerce with China. We need a railroad to do that though. What do you say?" He asks as he extends his hand over toward my tub.

I look him in the eyes and shake his hand. "I tell you what, you put a little bread in my pocket to throw at people and earn respect, you got a deal, Linc."

He smiles at me broadly. "How does ten grand sound to start? I'll keep sending more money after I get word you made it alive."

"That sounds like a fucking deal," I say with a huge smile.

We shake like old bros. It was an offer I couldn't resist, and more importantly, a chance to return to the financial status that I was accustomed to. Saint James Street James was getting his freedom back. I put the rest of the cigar out in my bath water and step out of the tub, looking down at him.

"You coming out when I finish?" I ask him.

"Of course. I'll be on the first train out as long as nothing crazy happens."

"Yeah, don't get your fucking head blown off out here," I say as we enjoy a long laugh together.

An older white man comes out an offers me a towel, which I decline, because I air dry. I put my cowboy hat and holster on, then walk out of the bath house buck naked. The sun felt nice on my skin as beads of water slapped off my dong as I walked down the street. My swagger is back. I am an important man again.

A carriage was waiting for me in town attached to my steed. In the back, I could see the coffin in which Daniel was in. An American flag was draped over it. It was a classy move. A Union soldier was waiting next to it with some fresh clothes for me too.

Abraham Lincoln was a first class motherfucker. I wouldn't be the man I am today without him, that's for goddamn sure.

I put the clothes on and hop up on my steed, with a couple Union soldiers escorting me on horseback behind me. Looking back at them, I motion for them to stop. I stare at Daniel's casket for a moment, before directing my attention to the men.

"Boys, I need to make one stop first," I say.

"Where to sir?" One of the soldiers asked.

"Virginia. I have to tell his wife that he died."

The two men look at each other and nod solemnly. I dig my spurs into my steed and we head back down south. It was the appropriate thing to do. Plus, after the sexual display I put on at Chantelle's, I figured she'd give me a freebie. Let's face it, I've earned it.

During the two-day journey down to Fredericksburg pulling a carriage with my deceased son in the back, I had a lot of time to think. It was mostly about myself, and whether or not I should keep my beard or lose it. Ultimately, I decided to keep it knowing that I'd have to deal with all these grimy motherfuckers building railroads. I needed them to respect me. In a hard labor sitch like that, they'd try and challenge a clean shaven Adonis like myself at every turn just to see if they could best me. Pulling into the driveway, I finally thought about Daniel and his wife.

I took a deep breath as I hop down from my steed and walk toward the front door of the house. This is going to be tough. I've never had to tell a wife that their husband is dead before. Usually I'm the one killing people and then other people deal with this shit. A million thoughts flooded my mind as I knock on the door. Penelope was obviously surprised to see me. I totally froze and just blurted out the first thing that came to my mind.

"Do you have any Cole slaw—your husband is dead!"

"What?"

"It's Daniel... he's dead. The Cole slaw was for me. I'm pretty hungry, I'm sorry. I don't know how to do this," I say.

She collapses on the ground and starts crying hysterically. "Why did you tell me like *that?*"

"Look, there really is no easy way to do this. It's been a long two days for me, besides fruit and nuts, I've had nothing else in my belly—

"No, why did you tell me about Daniel like this?"

I bend down and scoop her up, taking her into my arms. "What was I supposed say? Daniel has a surprise for you, but you have to go to the carriage—oops, sorry that surprise is death? I felt that would have been a little too much."

Penelope tries to regain herself. "What am I supposed to do now?"

"Well, you don't have any kids, so that's a bonus to a possible suitor. If it were me, I wouldn't even tell people you were ever married, that way you're not damaged goods on the open market."

"Lovely. I mean what am I supposed to do about a funeral?"

"I'll take care of that. He wanted to be buried next to his brothers and his mom," I say as I pull out the all nude portrait of Louretta and hold it up to her face. "He loved her so very much."

Penelope shakes her head and tries to wipe away her tears. Her makeup smears everywhere, and this beautiful girl, suddenly looks like shit. I decide not to say anything, but I definitely avoid eye contact.

Finally, she musters, "I want to go with you to California."

"What? Why?" I ask.

"I want to be there for his funeral. He was my entire life and I have to be there for his final goodbye," she says tearfully.

"Fuck. You can't. I just got this job building the transcontinental railroad. It's going to be a few months before I make it back that way. Will a body even keep that long?" I mutter to myself.

"Then I'm coming with you," she says defiantly.

"No, you're not. There's a real rough and tumble, surf and turf element out there. I don't want to be responsible for your death too," I say.

She looks at me stunned. "What do you mean *too*? Were you responsible for Daniel's death?"

I backtrack quickly, "I doubt it, but as a father, you always feel responsible. War is hell and there is no way I could have predicted his passing while I was having sex. I would have asked him to watch if I would have known."

"You're a horrible person," she says crying again, which continuously fucks up her make-up.

"Thank you. Now it's time for me to go," I say as I stand up and begin to walk back to the carriage.

"I'm still coming with you. I don't care what you say," she says, picking herself up off the ground.

"No. It's too dangerous," I say vigorously.

She pulls out a Derringer pistol that was strapped to her inner thigh and aims it at me. "I can handle myself. I'm a strong southern woman."

"How much can you curl? Give me pounds, not kilograms," I ask.

"It doesn't fucking matter because I can shoot," she says as she turns and fires her pistol at a stray bottle fifty yards away, shattering it. "Plus, I can cook, which means you'll *have something in your belly*," she says mocking me.

Goddamnit. Pinterest is right. You really can get to a man's dong by feeding him. I hope I'm not in violation by using that quote. I exhale loudly for twenty seconds and stare her down.

"Fine. You can ride in the back with the casket," I concede.

"Thank you. I'll grab my things," she says as she puts the gun away.

I nod my head and walk over to my steed as she heads inside the house. Once inside, I begin riding off immediately, but it turns out she's pretty fucking fast, and she catches up remarkably quick. Welcome to pulling a fucking carriage behind you. These goddamn things are slow as shit. Without slowing down, she's able to hop in the back of the carriage, sandwiching herself in tightly with the casket.

"You good back there?" I call out over my shoulder.

"You're the worst fucking person of all time," she screams as she tries to give herself some separation from the casket.

"I knew you'd make it. You're a whatever-the-fuck people say to encourage women to do shit type of gal," I say, genuinely not caring.

"Asshole," she chirps back.

I deliberately hit a pothole and the casket slams her violently against the wall of the carriage. Little did she know, I actually wasn't being an asshole. Instead I was trying to prepare her for the type of men who would be on this journey. These filthy fucks on the railroads would be way more hardcore than anything she's seen down south. I figured she might as well get used to it.

The Union soldiers ride up next me, "We'll take the lead from here. Anytime you want to stop for the night, just say so and we'll make camp," one of them says.

"Where are we headed anyway? Linc didn't say where this whole shit was kicking off," I say.

"Omaha, Nebraska. You ever been?" The other soldier asks.

"No. It sounds like a city you'd scream out to confuse people before throwing something at them."

They laugh. "They actually have great steaks there."

"I hope so. It better not be a bunch of people sitting around fucking ears of corn all goddamn day," I say as they continue to laugh and take the lead out front.

With the war still going on, we tried to stay clear of the action as best we could by traveling a little further north during our ride out west. The first night we ended up making camp in Ohio, which is a state. I'd elaborate further, but every state back then was pretty fucking boring. If you could avoid a bear rape, congrats, you probably had a decent trip.

As the sun was setting, Penelope began to cook a turkey that I blew the head off in the forest earlier, in a fire made by the two Union soldiers. Turns out Penelope actually was a good cook. She had that thing defeathered and mounted rotisserie style like we were in a goddamn Boston Market. One of the soldiers offers me a flask of whiskey, which I immediately take as my own. I even pull out a small buck knife and carve my initials into to it to be safe in case I put it down and forget.

"I appreciate the whiskey," I say in a suggestive tone letting them know they are not getting it back.

"It's an honor sir," he says, saluting me like he should.

"I know it is. What are your names?" I ask.

"I'm George and this is Lucas," he says, motioning to the other soldier.

"Beautiful stars out tonight," Lucas says.

"Small talk is for the vertically challenged. Why don't you ask me what you really want to ask me?" I demand.

George nudges Lucas nervously. "Okay. Did you really beat up President Lincoln? The other soldiers say you gave him a mighty whoopin'. Is that true, sir?" Lucas asks.

I give a thousand-yard stare into the distance and exhale deeply to once again add to the intrigue. Try it, it works. I do it all the time. "Well George, Lucas, a real man never talks about a fight, it would be disrespectful to his opponent and therefore prove him unworthy."

Lucas shakes his head understanding. "Of course. I'm sorry sir—

"Especially when that man was beaten over and over again until his face was almost unrecognizable, because there was so much blood. When you're punching a dude that hard and you're on the verge of caving in his skull with your fists—there really is no need to talk about it. Do you comprehend what I'm saying?"

All of their faces looked freaked the fuck out. Penelope has stopped turning the rotisserie stick. Finally, George pipes up.

"Uh, yeah, sure," he says timidly.

"Penelope, why don't you pick up the pace on that rotiss? I want that bird cooked even. Daniel wouldn't have had it any other way," I say making a twisting gesture with my hand.

Finally, she snaps out of it. "It's funny you say that. Daniel was the one who taught me how to cook poultry like this," she says as she smiles.

"Unless you guys used to double over together laughing while cooking poultry, I really don't see what's so funny?" I ask her confused.

"No, I just meant that he was the one who taught me this technique," she says as she looks at the ground.

"Well, he was certainly an expert in cooking domestic foul. He used to punch bald eagles out of the sky on opium as a kid and feed his family. I've never seen anything like it. That boy had a gift with birds I guess," I say reminiscing.

Penelope looks at me horrified. "You said that before dinner at our house. My Daniel actually used to punch bald eagles out of the sky and eat them?"

"Oh yeah. My dude was an expert. I'm surprised he never told you," I say as I tip back a long pull of whiskey not offering it to anyone else.

She shakes her head in disappointment. "I wonder what else he never told me," she says under her breath.

"Let's see, did he tell you he lost his virginity to an Asian prostitute at fourteen? Or the time he watched me during an orgy—

"That's enough. I think I'd rather just keep the memories I have of him," she says with sadness in her eyes.

"I completely understand. Is that fucking bird done? I'm so hungry I could put my dick inside it," I say rubbing my tum-tum.

She nods and begins to pull the turkey down from the flames, handing me the makeshift rotisserie stick. As I rip into the turkey like a rabid dog with a hookworm infection, tears well up in her eyes as she runs off toward the carriage. After one more huge mouthful, I hand the turkey off to the boys and give a light jog over to her, as she weeps next to Daniel's casket.

"You want us to save some for you?" I ask.

"I'm not hungry," she says through tears.

"I could box some up for you—shit, I'm sorry," I say as I tap the casket.

This causes her to cry even harder. I move toward her, but she pushes me away. "Can you just leave me alone for a minute please?"

"Look, I'm sorry. That's my son in there too. I'm also grieving pretty fucking hard," I say.

She turns angrily toward me, "Are you? Because you sure don't fucking seem like it. You've been nothing short of awful to me, his wife—

"If you're mad about me taking off in the carriage, it was a joke. I assumed you'd catch up eventually, and you did," I say with a kind smile.

"It's not just the carriage, it's everything. I feel like after all the horrible things you were saying that I didn't even *really* know him," she says wiping tears from her face.

"How *did* you know him?"

"What?" She asks exasperated.

"What kind of man was he to you?" I ask.

"He was—he was the kindest, most loyal man I've ever met in my life. The kind of man who would do anything for you at the drop of a hat. He was gentle, and sweet, and loving. Daniel was the exact opposite of everything you were saying about him earlier."

"Look, about that stuff I said—well it was true, but those were one offs. It was probably me being a bad father. I was the one who gave him opium, okay? I was the one who took him to the whorehouse, because I wished my dad had done that for me. Was it the right move? Probably. But everything else you said about Daniel is the real him. He was a great son. Shit, if I'm being real, he was my favorite out of all of them. He was brave. He had heart. He was everything I could've asked for in a son."

She finally cracks a smile through her tears. "Then why is he gone?"

"Only the good die young," I reply.

"What does that even mean?" She asks.

"I don't know, I heard it from some bullshit piano player in a bar once. I can't wait until that fad dies. Those guys are annoying as shit. Anyway, Daniel was a better man than me. God tends to take them first."

She nods gently, then leans in to hug me. I really don't believe in God or any of that shit, but I could tell in that moment that's what she needed to hear. The fact that she cared about my son that much and wasn't a complete whore meant a lot to me. Any woman who would travel cross country with a dead body in her lap for a few months is alright in my book. *Literally.* Because I am the author of this book.

I glance over to the fire where I see the two Union soldiers nod their heads in respect toward me for handling this situation with grace and humility. I return the favor by making the slashing of the throat gesture with my index finger across my neck, then pointing at the turkey letting them know I'll fucking kill them if they polish it off without me. They understood and put the stick against a rock by the fire, keeping it warm for me.

Chapter 9

INCH NAILS INTO THE FUCKING GROUND

After our little chat, the rest of the ride toward Omaha went pretty smoothly between Penelope and I. Hell, I was even actually enjoying the scenery... until we came across a bunch of dead white men hanging from trees in Iowa. That will really fuck up your afternoon. I halt my steed and draw my pistol, before leaping down for a closer inspection.

I pull a bandana out of my pocket and cover my nose and mouth as I inch closer to the bodies. Flies were swarming around them like hippies at a disc golf course in the summer. Their testicles were chopped off and made into wrist bouquets with actual flowers and baby's breath tied to their hands. It was brutal, yet somehow poignant. George and Lucas leap down from their

157

horses and draw their guns as we could hear Indians hollering out in the distance.

"Stay in the carriage Penelope!" I yelled back.

Fucking Indians are ruthless man. Straight fucking savage. I begin to survey the land with the binoculars I stole from Stonewall Jackson. Yeah, of course I took those fuckers. A sweet set of binocs back in the day was like having a dope set of Ray Bans during *Coachella*. There was no way I *wasn't* stealing those things. After witnessing what was actually happening in the tree side off to my left, I'm glad I did take them, or I would have been fucked.

The hollering was coming from a set of Sioux Indians as they scalped what appeared to be ten white settlers. Whether they were just passing through or trying to take the Indians land, I couldn't tell you. What I can tell you is that one of the Indians was making a necklace out of human toupees and I for goddamn sure didn't want my beautiful mane to be the centerpiece of their latest halter neck chain. George and Lucas grab their pistols, asking if they have permission to start shooting. I shake my head and motion for them to stand down.

I needed to think. Twenty Indians at this distance with the weapons we had sure the fuck wasn't going to cut it. They were too far for rifle reloads between all of us, and if we rode up on them, their arrows would take us out before we could kill them all. Obviously, I had some experience with Indians in the past, but this was a different land and the country was heading in a different direction. That direction was, "Hey bro's, we're going to take all your shit and leave you with nothing except a few professional sports mascots in the future."

They knew it, and I knew it. I look over at Penelope who is visibly shaken as she sits quietly in the back of the carriage, clutching her Derringer. In that moment there was only one thing I could do, which was to go completely fucking indigenous. I rip off my shirt and walk back over to George and Lucas. They each stare at me with a look of confusion.

"I need your hat, George," I say in a quiet tone.

"Sure," he says as he takes off his hat and hands it to me quickly.

"Thanks," I say as I take it and begin to unzip my pants.

Without breaking eye contact with him, I begin to take the longest piss of my entire adult life into his hat. People have run the 400-meter dash faster than it took for me to stop this stream. I was well over a minute, but every drop was a necessity. When I finished, my body quivered with the same exultation of a new born polar bear getting adjusted to the snow for the first time. I then carefully place the hat on the ground to ensure not one single drop escapes.

"You just pissed in my hat. What the fuck are you doing?" George asks.

"Becoming one of them. We're outmatched in this fight. This is the only way to get us out of here," I say as I begin to take off my boots and pants.

"That still doesn't answer the question of why you used *my* hat? Why couldn't you use your own—and why the fuck are you taking off your pants?" George asks in a hushed tone.

"Because I have the stones to," I say as I reach down and pick up two lime stones off the ground and rub them together over the hat.

The lime stones slowly begin to crumble into the urine soaked hat. Once the stones have completely disintegrated and dissolved into my own piss, I walk over and snap off a branch from the closest tree. I take the stick and begin carefully stirring the two elements until a chalky white mixture starts to form.

Once I'm satisfied with the proper texture, I throw the stick to the side and begin applying the mixture to my body. I coat every square inch of myself in it until I have the same applicant as the Indians. There's just one thing missing: war paint. I debate cutting one of the soldiers, but the Indians would notice if they got close that one of my men was bleeding. I needed something else. My eyes turn toward Penelope.

I walk over to the carriage and stop at the door. "Do you have any feathers from the turkey I shot the other night?"

"Of course. I made a dream catcher later on that night to ward off any evil spirits that might be lurking," she says.

"How'd that work out? Such a basic white girl move," I say as I rip the dream catcher down from the inner roof of the carriage. I take her scarf off from around her neck and tear it in half.

"Hey! That's my scarf!"

"And it might save your life," I say as I begin to tie the feathers around my head with her scarf. "I'm also going to need something else."

"Fine. What?" She asks annoyed.

"Are you on your period?" I say as I point to her vagina.

"Excuse me?"

"Are you menstruating? I really need to know."

She shakes her head begrudgingly. "Yes."

"I know. You've been pissed off the whole day. I'm going to need some."

"Some of what?" She asks dumbfounded.

"Some of that sex ketchup. When I look away, I need you to insert two fingers inside of you, then apply the blood to my face underneath my eyes."

"You can't be serious?" She asks in defiance.

161

"I'm afraid I am. It's a matter of life and death."

With the Indians hollering growing louder and louder in the background, she takes a deep breath and closes her eyes. "Fine. I want you to know, that I will never forget this," she says.

"Neither will I, obviously," I say as I give the old Jon Cena motion to my face.

"Turn away," she says disgusted.

I oblige and turn my head, closing my eyes. A few seconds later I feel her two fingers rubbing warm blood underneath my eyes. My transformation is complete. I stare at her and nod my head, letting her know she did the right thing. Then I tell her.

"You did the right thing," I say sincerely.

"Fuck off," she seethes.

And with her vote of confidence, I motion for George and Lucas to saddle up as I mount my steed.

"Resume riding behind me as if this is any other fucking day," I instruct them.

"So you want us to pretend that you're not covered in your own urine and someone's period blood?" George asks.

"Remind me to wash it off in your sarcasm after I save your life. Keep your fucking mouths shut when we approach," I say over my shoulder as we ride.

Within twenty to thirty seconds of resuming our ride through, the Indians to the right of me on top of the hill spot us and begin to charge with tomahawks. I maintain my cool and continue to ride as if nothing is going on. I'm somehow able to maintain a steady heart rate, although the stench from my own urine is really starting to get to me. Turns out Penelope threw a dash of asparagus into her turkey seasoning yesterday, and now I'm paying the ultimate price.

The Indians surround us within seconds, shaking their tomahawks violently in our faces. They stare at me in confusion, as a few of them begin circling me slowly. I can tell they are trying to figure me out, but they can't. A couple of them huddle up around the eldest Indian and begin to whisper amongst themselves. After a brief discussion, the eldest Indian steps out in front of the pack.

I hop down from my steed, which causes immediate panic amongst them. Hollering ensues in a heated exchange as they inch closer. In this moment, I could not show fear. Having been raped by twenty hot Indian women as a boy, I felt confident I could communicate with them.

The following conversation actually took place in Sioux, but I'm not even going to bother to write that bullshit out. You dummies wouldn't understand anyway. I'm a rape survivor, so it stuck with me.

"I come in peace," I say.

"You will leave in pieces," the eldest one exclaims.

"Not very original. I have been paid a large sum of money to escort these whites across this land to bury their dead son in California."

They seem skeptical. "Why do you have turkey feathers in your hair? That symbolizes nothing," he hisses.

"You know white people, if I don't do the whole song and dance, they won't think I'm real and won't pay for this shit."

This elicits a few chuckles from some of the other Indians, but the eldest does not seem amused. He begins circling me extremely close, sniffing my skin. He recoils from the scent.

"What is your name?" He asks.

"*Erection-Won't-Go-Down.* It stems from a problem I've had since I was a child," I say as I point down to my now enormous boner covered in white paint.

This elicits even more laughter, as well as a few sexual glances from some of the other Indians. More importantly, it proved to them that in the face of imminent danger, my adrenaline is on such a max level that I'm able to maintain an erection. There is nothing more dangerous in this world than a man with a murder boner. I had reached maximum ketosis, and my one hundred percent all beef thermometer purveyed that.

"Prove your Indian skills to me," the eldest says in a challenging tone.

"How so?" I ask.

"Tomahawk. I go first," he says as he turns rapidly and fires his tomahawk thirty yards down hill at a painted target.

Whack!

Direct hit, center target. The rest of his tribe nods impressed, as the eldest Indian turns back toward me and gets right up in my face. We are now nose to nose, neither us blinking. I extend my hand out to the closest Indian next to him.

"Give me four Tomahawks," I demand.

"Four?" He asks, looking at the eldest Indian for approval. He nods giving him the go ahead.

Two other Indians step forward and give me their tomahawks. I take a couple steps back to my steed and open up my saddle bag, pulling out four apples. They stare at me with confusion.

"White people, get down from your horses. White woman, get out of your carriage," I instruct in broken English to try and throw the Indians off.

"What the hell are you doing?" the eldest Indian asks.

"Proving my Indian skills," I say as I dip back into Sioux.

George, Lucas, and Penelope look at me with frightened faces as I line them up next to my steed. One by one, I place the apples on top of their heads—including my steed. I walk back twenty paces and see their eyes frozen in panic. Initially, I wasn't sure if it was because of my erection, or the fact that I was going to throw tomahawks at them. It was probably a mixture of both.

"Hold still white people, or you will die too," I say reverting back to broken English.

George looks at Lucas and whispers, "Holy. Fucking. Shit."

"We're going to fucking die," I can hear Lucas whisper back.

They all close their eyes and stiffen their bodies as tightly as they can as I take a deep breath and steady my nerves. "One, two, three—

I spin and launch all four tomahawks at the same time. Those few seconds of flight seem like a lifetime as everyone watches them fly through the air. Simultaneously, all four apples split in half as the tomahawks sail past them. The Indians turn and holler impressed. The eldest was clearly pissed he had been outdone. George and Lucas were also clearly pissed, because I could see a steady stream rolling down each of their pant legs. My steed winks at me, he knows I am a fucking boss like that.

I walk back over to my horse, knowing I needed something else to appease the eldest Indian. He was obviously their leader, and although I had put my bravado on display in stunning fashion, I still need to get everyone out of here alive. That's when I had to pull out my go-to: the venerable Asian opium pipe that the old Chinaman had given me back home.

When I pull it out and walk it over to the eldest Indian, *ooh's and ahh's* were audibly heard from the tribe. This fucking pipe translated to *every* culture. They have never seen anything like this before. A few of them even rub their fingers across it trying to figure out the texture and detail. I nod and hand it to the eldest.

"A peace offering," I said with a warm smile, flawlessly transitioning to Sioux.

He still seems miffed, but after momentary hesitation, he eventually agrees. "Okay, but we pack it with *my* offering," he says, matching my smile.

"Of course," I agree.

He arches his brow, seemingly satisfied, and runs back to his teepee to grab his shit. It took everything in me to contain my laughter. Come on. I know this fucking game. It's the classic "my shit is better than your's and it will really mess you up man" mentality. A tale as old as time. The problem with that is, Saint James Street James doesn't give a fuck. Bring your bullshit weed over and let's shrub the fuck up, son.

Moments later he returns with a pouch full of weed and begins packing my bowl. I obviously neglect to tell him that I've been smoking opium out of that pipe for years, so good luck with that residue kickback off your forest shit *Kemosabe*. He hands the glass dick back to me fully packed, then sits down on the ground *his* style and starts to rub two sticks together to create fire, which took fucking forever.

I would have just grabbed the matches in my saddle bag, but Indians refused to use matches back then, so I didn't want to give myself away. Instead, I stood there for thirty-five minutes until a tiny spark was finally made and he was able to catch a leaf on fire. He then lit my pipe, and I took a massive inhale leaving him very little fire on the leaf. I quickly hand the pipe back to him, leaving him with no choice but to take a rip before the fire went out.

The eldest Indian tries to match my pull, but that ope-dog kicker hits him too hard. He coughs all over the place like a hamster with tuberculosis. His face begins to sweat and his head starts swaying. When one of his eyes drifted off like Forrest Whitaker, I knew I had him. I grabbed my pipe and smiled warmly as I got up, motioning for George, Lucas, and Penelope to get back to our horses and carriage.

"Thank you for your generous hospitality. I shall cherish this encounter on my journey west," I say as I walk over to my steed.

He struggles to form a sentence, but he eventually blurts out in a delayed slur, "Wait!"

I turn back. "Yes?"

"You didn't exhale?" He asks exasperated.

"I never do. Enjoy your evening," I say as I turn and hop up onto my steed.

George and Lucas quickly got back on their horses, as Penelope slammed the door to her carriage. As we were riding out, I see the eldest Indian try to stand up, but he couldn't. He just keeps falling over like a drunk sorority sister desperately trying to hit the play button on her Bose Soundtouch for her Katy Perry playlist after a breakup. The rest of his tribe roars in laughter as he attempts to make it to his feet. We didn't stay long enough to see if he ever did.

Once we were clear of their territory, George and Lucas ride up along side of me. They seem to be really out of it. Maybe they were still paralyzed in fear. Maybe they were pissed off about the impromptu tomahawk/apple sesh. Who knows. I finally look back and glare at them.

"What the fuck bro?" I ask George.

"Do you mind if we stop up here for the night and find some place to camp?" he says with weary eyes.

"It seems a little sudden to be honest. Probably make more sense to put some more miles between us and those Indians," I say as I keep riding.

"That's what you said seven days ago," Lucas says.

"What? I don't know what you're talking about?" I ask confused.

"We've been riding for seven days straight following you. We haven't slept. *You* haven't slept. Neither of us can keep this pace up much longer," Lucas says exhausted.

I dig my heels into the ribs of my steed, and that's when I realize that I'm not wearing any boots. As a matter of fact, I'm still half painted like an Indian and my feet are dirty as shit. Holy fuck man. I have to stop doing hallucinogens*. This is the second time in the last couple months this has now happened where I've blanked out on multiple days. Classic Saint James. I can't help but chuckle to myself.

I look over at the boys and nod. "Yeah, I guess we can make camp for the night somewhere around here. Just listen for a stream will you? I'm dirty as shit and I could really use a bath."

They nod in agreement. Whether they were relieved that we were finally stopping, or simply relieved that I was finally showering, I'll never have that answer. I didn't want to let them know that I was tripping for seven days straight, so I let them find a spot.

A few miles up we halted our horses near a large stream. I headed down toward the water as the men begin to start a fire. While I was cleaning myself in the chilly water, I finally start to regain my cognitive senses. My eyes focus back to normal at the

---

* I've said the same thing my entire adult life regarding hallucinogens. Spoiler alert: I never stopped doing them.

sight of the big bright moon above me. About twenty feet down stream, I notice a small beaver trudging through the water.

"Would you mind looking the other way? I have to rinse off too, asshole," a nude Penelope said to me in a super annoyed tone.

"I'm sorry. I didn't mean to stare. I was just making sure you weren't going to drown," I say quickly trying to cover.

"The water is about four feet deep. I think I'll be able to navigate it," she says sternly.

"Well, a child could die in three inches of bath water, so it's better to be safe than a dead baby," I say as I turn around, respecting her private parts.

Penelope swims over to within five yards of me. Her body is submerged in water and she doesn't know that the moon light is blasting her perky tits into 4K for my peepers. Man, that fucking moon has always had my back. Penelope does that thing that people do when they're trying to pretend to tread water which is too shallow to make sense.

"Look, I never got to thank you for what you did back there with those Indians a week ago."

"No need. That was just me being a man," I say.

"Oh, okay. Because I was screaming for you—and either you couldn't hear me or you just wouldn't stop—anyway, I wanted to thank you now."

"A decent meal and some fresh clothes is all the thanks I need," I say.

"Sounds good. I'll wash your other clothes while you hunt for dinner," she says in a friendlier tone.

I jam both my hands deep into the stream and pull up four huge fish and immediately hold them skyward. "I'm done hunting. I'll meet you fireside," I say as I walk out of the stream.

She nods impressed. "That was incredible."

"Maybe to some," I say as I don't bother looking back.

The four of us lie near the fire enjoying the last few bites of our fish while my steed lays behind me as I use his body for a headrest. I feed him an apple as I discard the rest of my fish carcass into the fire and look over at the men, who seem a little more rejuvenated now that they have some food in them.

"George, Lucas, how was your meal? There's nothing like fresh fish straight from the stream," I say with a wink.

"Um, it was good. Is there any reason you're still not wearing any clothes?" George asks.

"Oh, yeah, Penelope said she was going to freshen some up for me. Have you seen her? She didn't drown fake swimming did she?"

"I'm not sure what you're talking about, but I saw her back by the carriage a few minutes ago," Lucas says.

"Thanks," I say as I stand up and walk back over there, picking up her plate of fish to bring to her.

I've never been sure of carriage etiquette as it pertains to a living space. Do you knock on the door? Pull back the curtain? I'm not real cultured on it, so I just rip open the fucking door and let myself in. Penelope turns away somewhat startled, as she finishes buttoning the top of her blouse.

"Sorry, you scared me. I was just—

"Putting your tits away? It's fine. I brought you a plate of fish. I hope you like pan seared, because that's how you made it," I say handing her the plate.

She smiles genuinely. "Thank you. Here," she says as she turns and hands me a fresh set of folded clothes. "They might be a little damp still. I'd recommend leaving them out overnight to dry by the fire."

"Unfortunately, I can't. I need something to cover this," I say as I point down to my enormous erection.

"Oh my God, you still have that. Wow. I have a quilt for you, if you want to wrap yourself in it for the night and let your clothes dry," she says as she hands me the quilt.

"Thank you. That's very kind," I say as I cover myself up in it. "What are these little tiny horns embroidered on it?" I ask, looking down at what appears to be small brass trumpets sewn in.

"Those are actually hearing aids. I used to teach at a school for the deaf back in Fredericksburg," she says wistfully.

I can tell how much she misses teaching. "Well, it's a beautiful aids quilt. I am *positive* that I will take good care of it. Have a good night's sleep. According to George and Lucas, we should be at our destination tomorrow."

"That's great. I guess it was smart of you to keep moving for seven days straight after all," she says.

I look away, "Yup, that was my sole intention of doing that. Time is the devil's split oyster my grandfather never said. Anywho, have a great—

"Um, do you want to stay and have a drink? I have some plum wine stashed away in my bag. I was saving it for—

"A family member coming out as homosexual? I'm kidding. I'd love some," I say as I squeeze inside the back of the carriage next to her, behind the casket.

She takes out a small, old wooden barrel out of a bag and pulls the cork from inside the top. I hold it up to a lantern that she has set on top of the casket and examine it. There's an inscription on the the barrel that reads; ***Captain Barefoot, 1772 Ireland.***

I take a huge swig. "Oh shit, this is harder than I thought. I'm sorry about the gay comment earlier, this is definitely no homo."

I wipe my mouth and hand the tiny barrel back to her and she takes a drink. "It's almost one hundred years old. We were saving it to celebrate when Daniel and I had our first child, but obviously that didn't happen. It's been in my family for years," she says.

"Forgive me, I'm not that familiar with Barefoot wine," I say inquisitively.

"It's not that famous. My great-grandfather was a pirate from Ireland, he didn't want it to be too commercial. He used to make it for drinking on long journeys when he sailed around Europe and killed people," she says taking another swill.

"He sounds like a great man," I say as she takes yet another pull. "Whoa, you better slow down on that. That stuff has quite the kick."

"I come from a long line of pirates, I'm sure I'll be fine. You're kind of a pirate too, wouldn't you say?" She asks with a smirk.

"Sort of, I guess. Most might call me a natural born killer, a deft vagabond, a scrappy chimney sweep, a vagina thief, a goose whisperer—it's tough to say what people identify with the most, you know?"

The flame inside the lantern begins to dance as one of the men outside starts to play the harmonica softly. I can feel Penelope staring at me, as I take a deep pull of the Barefoot wine and feel it burn in my belly. This shit is no easy sip. I can feel her retinas studying me like an eye chart.

"You keep stealing glances from me and one of these times I'm not going to give them back," I say.

She turns and blushes. "I'm sorry, it's just—I was thinking about—

"My erection from earlier? I know. We can't obviously," I say as I pour a little bit of wine out on top of the casket for Daniel.

"Obviously. That would be crazy, right?" she says as she leans into me resting her face against mine.

I close my eyes and whisper, "Goddamnit Penelope. I'm trying here. I'm really fucking trying. I don't want to be disrespectful to Daniel's memory."

She takes the wine from my hands seductively and takes one last chooch. "*Or* are we honoring his memory by keeping the family name still alive? We never did conceive. That's what this wine was meant for after all."

I take the wine right back from her and take an enormous chug. "Don't you fucking do this to me, Penelope—I can't—say no right now. This fucking Barefoot has me like—

"Whoa? Me too. I just need a man right now so bad," she whispers with desperation.

"What about the two by the fire?" I ask.

176

"The fudge brothers? I don't get down with those limp wrists. I need you to take me right now, or I'm taking it from you," she says as she puts her hand underneath the aids quilt, grabbing my cock.

"You're probably going to need your other hand as well," I whisper as I grab her other digits and place them on my shaft.

She grabs my dick like an out of work lumberjack who had just been given an ax for the first time in months. I knock the lantern out of the tiny window of the carriage and throw her down on top of the casket, tearing her clothes off. She arches her back and I pour out the remaining contents of plum wine all over her body before insertion. I begin making love to her while lapping up the wine off her breasts like a St. Bernard.

I hear the harmonica briefly stop outside, and I yell out, "KEEP FUCKING PLAYING! DON'T YOU FUCKING STOP UNTIL I DO!"

The harmonica immediately fires back up. As I penetrate her deeper and deeper, I see her fingers reach above her head and latch on top of the casket for momentum. It suddenly dawns on me that this is the second dead son of mine whose casket I have now had sex on. Jesus. What the fuck is wrong with me?

Obviously, I don't stop at this point, but over the course of the next two hours—it does hit me that I have some sort of sickness. Or maybe *they* were in the wrong place at the wrong time? It's your simple chicken before the egg scenario as far as I'm concerned. Either way, I decide to pull out at the last second, because it would be too fucked up to impregnate my deceased son's wife. Let's face it, there definitely would have been a baby after this.

Ultimately, I end with a sweet finishing move on her tits. It was the classy way to go. Although she seems a tad disappointed, she understands. I wrap myself up in the quilt and exit the carriage, taking a seat down at the fire with George and Lucas, one of which has now stopped playing harmonica.

"Who the fuck was playing the harm like that during my fuck sesh?" I ask.

George pulls the harmonica out of his pocket sheepishly and holds it up. "It was me."

I grab it from him, wiping the grill of it off on my quilt. "You were about two octaves low on those songs for the last two hours. Here's how they should have been played."

I put the harm to my lips and begin playing with the expertise he should have. Why did I decide to do this right now? One, you should never be to busy to teach. Two, just fucking kidding, I didn't care about teaching this asshole anything. I did it because I didn't want Penelope to hear a bunch dudes talk to me about what it was like balling out the widow. I wanted her to be able to have some peace of mind that I wasn't a complete dirtbag. Also, let's say I'm window shopping again and decide to go in and make another purchase someday, I didn't want to sully this. You get it.

The following morning, we rise just after dawn and begin to head out toward the Nebraska Territory. The rest of the ride was relatively relaxing. I hadn't seen Penelope that happy the entire time. That's what a good dicking does. She even joined me up front for the last hundred miles. Everything was peaceful, until we passed by the sign that read: **Omaha.**

Upon arrival in Omaha, Nebraska it was every bit as fucking grungy as Abraham Lincoln had described. It reminds me of my old mining town from home back in the day, except this time, there was a bunch of filthy motherfuckers working on a railroad instead of inside a gold mine. I now understood why he wanted me for the job. This type of labor needed a man with hubris. One who wasn't afraid to take charge and earn some fucking respect.

"Stay here, Penelope," I instruct as I halt my steed.

When I hop down from my four-legger, I stretch and survey the landscape. Men of all ages were hammering in nine inch spikes into railroad tracks, most of them of Chinese descent. Off in the distance, I see an older white man in his fifties with a huge beard, kicking an exhausted and sweaty Chinaman on the ground.

When the Chinaman couldn't take the punishment anymore, the white guy began to take off his belt, wrapping it around his palm. Shit, I knew exactly what the fuck was about to go down. I walk over to George and Lucas, who wince as the whipping commenced.

"You guys can take off," I say.

Judging by their reactions to the beating that ensues, they seem surprised. "Are you sure you don't want help?" Lucas asked.

"I'm sure. I got it from here boys, this is my world. Tell that honest son of a bitch I'm indebted to him." I then shook their hands, genuinely grateful for their company.

As I was walking away, George called out to me, "Hey Street? It's been a pleasure to know the finest outlaw on United States soil."

I turn back and smile. "You probably should have said worldwide. Time to do what I do best and start stackin' bodies again."

With the tip of my cowboy hat, I spin on my heels and head straight for the older white man whipping the Asian, who is now lying face down, bleeding profusely. I slide back the side of my duster jacket with my right hand as I prepare to go for my pistol. Time to get wet.

"You there, stop whipping that Chinaman," I say sternly.

He turns and spits out a huge stream of tobacco juice. In a voice like Sam Elliott he asks, "And who the fuck are you?"

"I'm Saint James Street James. I hate road abbreviations so I pronounce my last name. Right now, you're whipping up one of my workers pretty good, and I say he's had enough."

"One of your's? You have some fucking nerve—

"And I also have the backing of the President of the United States, Mr. Abraham Lincoln. I'm to oversee the building of this railroad now," I say without batting an eye.

He looks at me enraged and goes for his pistol. "Over my dead—

"Fine," I say quickly.

Bang!

I don't even let him get out the word "body" before dropping this motherfucker dead in front of everybody. There isn't a better way of showing dominance than by blowing away the man formerly in charge in your first five minutes on the job. I walk over to his dead body and a grab the nearest Chinaman next to him and point to him.

"Who is this man I killed?" I ask.

The Chinaman stuttered in broken English. "He works for the wailwoad company. Hasn't been paying us."

I nod my head. "Is this why he was beating this man?" I say as I point to the other Chinaman lying face down on the ground.

"Yes. He stood up for us and then," he begins to make a whipping motion, obviously not knowing the word.

I walk over to the man to see if he is still alive. Kneeling down, I slowly roll him over and hear him gurgling up blood. He shields his eyes from the sun as he looks up at me, face covered in dirt and blood, barely able to speak.

"Saint James, I knew you would come find me," he says hardly able to whisper.

I take the Chinaman's canteen off his neck and pour some water over his face. When the dirt and blood start to dissipate, I can recognize his face plain as day. It's Samantha Davis. Son of a bitch.

Chapter 10

MY ASIAN GANG IS ALL BACK TOGETHER

December 5th, 1863
Omaha, Nebraska

As the sun begins to set, Samantha and I sit around a campfire. Sam's face is badly beaten, but he's alive. This guy is a goddamn fighter. At this point, I can't even tell you how many times he's been fucked up this bad. His will to live is absolutely miraculous.

I light up a fresh heater as Penelope walks over with warm bowls of stew for all of us. Samantha takes a sip and rests his back against the wagon wheel of the carriage. He smiles, and I can see that once again, his teeth are broken. This guy's dental luck is insane.

"I'm so happy to see you Saint James," he says with that old lisp I'm accustomed to.

"You too my friend. What have you been up to these last few years, except the obvious of working for slave's wages again," I say with a chuckle.

"Well, I went as far east as I could without getting near the civil war. Americans treat us Chinese below black people here, but slightly above Indians," he says rather upbeat.

"At least you're winning at something," I say as I sip my stew.

"We ran out of money so we joined the railway construction. We get thirty dollars a month and food."

"Wait you get thirty bucks a month? That's like twenty times more than I was paying you," I say in astonishment.

"Trust me, there isn't one white person who wants this job. Even I was shocked," he says, somehow able to laugh through his fucked up situation.

His laughter on this subject is infectious, and I can't help but share a guffaw with him. "So what's the skinny on this whole sitch? Who was the motherfucker that I just killed?"

"He works for the railroad company. They are the ones with the real power. He walks around doing whatever he wants. At least he used to," he says trying to smile.

"Well I'm here now, so shit is going to change. I mean, you're obviously still going to work for me and whatnot, but I know how hard you guys grind. I'll stay out of your assholes. Any of the old crew here with you?" I ask.

"All of dem." Samantha then tries to whistle, but it's really shitty, so I whistle for him. Within seconds of my signal, all of my old Chinamen pop their heads up down the rail line and wave. Fuckin' A. They don't even forget a whistle.

"Who's the girl?" He asks as he points to Penelope hovering over the fire, now pouring herself a bowl of stew.

"That's Daniel's ex-wife," I say.

"Wait he was married before he got killed by the Marshals?" He asks confused.

"Long story, but he turned out to be alive somehow, got married, then he got re-killed. It's really fucked up. His body is in a casket in the carriage. We're taking him back to California after this."

"Did you have sex with her?" He asks, now attempting a half smile.

I slap him hard across the face. "What? No. Of course not. I would never have sex with my dead son's wife. Jesus man."

Samantha picks himself back up like nothing happened. "Okay. By the way, are you staying here?"

"Yeah. I was appointed by President Lincoln to oversee this project, so I'm in this for the long haul," I say taking a puff off my cig.

"No shit? The president himself?" He asks in amazement.

"Yup. Saint James Street James is on the straight and narrow."

We stare at each other for five seconds and then immediately burst out laughing. I punch him in the gooch, "I'm kidding! I'm still going to kill who ever I want under any circumstances!"

Samantha coughs up blood from the nut shot I just gave him as Penelope walks over. She looks down at him concerned. "Is he okay?"

"He's fine. Just a gooch shot is all. Samantha, this is Penelope."

Penelope looks at him curiously as she extends her hand. "I'm sorry, did you say Samantha?"

"Indeed I did. It's an amazing story that you'll have to hear another time," I say as I peer over the top of the fire towards town. "What's this town like Sam?"

"A lot like our old town in California. Very Wild West from what my squirrel di guy says," he says before taking another sip of stew.

"Shit man, they have squirrel di here? Hot fucking damn!" I throw my bowl of stew on the ground and grab Penelope's hand.

"I just made that," she says, annoyed.

"And that's great, but they have squirrel di here, so make yourself presentable. We're going into town milk faucets."

"What the hell is *squirrel di*?" She asks.

"It's more than five squirrel dicks thoroughly cooked over a fire. Extremely delicious. Throw some paint on the barn and let's head into town," I say as I clap my hands in excitement, accidently knocking her bowl out of her hand on to the ground in front of Samantha.

I'm sure he's had enough anyway. Penelope shakes her head as she walks over and climbs up into the carriage. I glance over at Samantha, who is now trying to scrape up Penelope's bowl of stew off the ground into his empty one. It's just a big pile of mud.

"What time do you guys usually get going in the morning?" I ask.

"Right around six," he says.

"AM? Fuck that. If you're married to that time, just keep it down, okay?" I say as I shake my head.

"Sure. I'll tell the others to hammer the huge steel spikes into the ground really quietly," he says.

I look down at him, trying to decipher if he was being sarcastic. He looks like he's near tears over the spilt stew, so I let it go. I head over to the fire and dump out the remaining stew into a bowl and put it in front of my steed.

"Eat up big fella, we're heading into town," I say to him as Samantha falls face down in the dirt from the affects of something I'm done trying to care about.

An hour later after Penelope was finally finished getting ready, we rode into town together on my steed. I was surprised how similar it was to my old mining town. Large wooden buildings with wooden boardwalk-style sidewalks lined the streets. The only brick structure was occupied by *The Herald*, which was their bullshit local newspaper. Ron would have creamed his fucking jeans to work in there. It was massive compared to the rinky-dink hole in the wall that he worked at. I wonder if somewhere he's sitting on his sewn-on penis thinking of me. I'm sure he is.

The storefronts were bustling with people coming in and out of jewelers, gun dealers, harness shops, and corrals. Hell, the town even had a hotel, which was unexpected. You can bet your sweet kitten dick I was laying my balls down on that thing while I stayed here. All in all, this place wasn't that bad. The funny thing about camp towns that had somehow happened upon mining and railways, is that people just laid down a makeshift downtown over what was already there.

The rest of Omaha was farmland and prairies, with just this big fucking town dropped in the middle. I'm certainly not going to bitch about it after spending the last five or so years sleeping in tents and barns across the nation. I'll take a hotel next to a good whorehouse any day of the week. As a matter of fact, it even felt like home. I spotted a sign above a bar that said "Billiards" on it and moseyed on over. I tie up my steed and help Penelope down as darkness began to fall. Obviously, I didn't catch it. Wink.

When we walked in, the stench of whiskey and awful perfume hit me smack across the face, and I enjoyed the shit out it. I escort Penelope to the bar and order two shots of their finest alligator char from the keep. She looks at me surprised as the bartender poured our whiskey.

"Is this a date?" She asks expectantly.

I waited five minutes then replied, "Would you like it to be?"

"Well, I'd be lying if I said it hadn't been awhile since a man has taken me out on the town."

"Then let's really go for it tonight. Dinner, jewels, you can find a friend and I can put you both in an ox yoke while I take turns from behind—

"Hang on. I'm sorry, but I'm just not that type of woman," she says quickly cutting me off.

"Oh, yeah, that's right. Sorry, it has been a long time for me too I guess—you know—with a *non-whore*. It's really hard to find a nonnie you just enjoy spending an evening with."

"Look, don't get me wrong, I'm into some kinky shit, just not with another stranger," she says taking a sip of her whiskey.

I nod and down my entire shot and slam it down, motioning the bartender to come over. "No, I understand. My dead wife was the same way. She was a good woman and only got down with strangers once. Even then, they technically weren't strangers, since they worked for me on my property."

"So I've heard. Daniel said he was watching that night," she says looking away.

"Sorry, that was just me being an awesome father," I say, thinking back to that night.

I once again pull out the fully nude portrait of her and lean it up against a glass on the bar, staring at it, momentarily lost in thought. "She was from Ireland as well, so there would be nights where I'd get naked, cut out two leg holes in a burlap sack, and she'd play the 'find the missing potatoes' game for hours. She was a special one," I say caressing the picture.

"I get that, but you could probably put the portrait away now. People are starting to stare," she says as she covers half her face.

"That's a beautiful bush man," a burly drunk guy in his forties leans over and says to me as he cries.

I can't help but acknowledge him, "Thank you."

"Reminds me of my Aunt," he says overcome with emotion as he gets up and leaves.

I take the picture off the bar and fold it up, putting it back in my pocket. Out of the corner of my eye I spot a faro table. I check my pocket to see how much cash I have on me. Plenty of jack to party.

"Let's make a real night of this, shall we?" I say to Penelope. "I'll be right back."

She looks at me intrigued as I get up and head to the faro table. An older gentleman who looks like an eyewear salesman, deals out cards as others walk up and play ahead of me. For those of you who don't know what faro is, it's the 1800's equivalent of fucking *Uno*. They basically just turn cards over and if you have a higher card, congrats you win money! As I approach, an older man walks off dejectedly after a loss. The faro dealer tries to spark up a convo with me.

"Howdy sir, can I fancy you in a game of chance?" He asks giddy as shit.

"A game of chance would be a reverse glory hole with your ass pressed up against the hole," I say.

"How would that work?" He asks with disgust.

"It's either going to be a cock or a tongue you're taking to the pooper, one can be pleasant, the other not-so-much."

"Gross," he says, really thinking about it.

"So is this fake conversation. Just pull a card, Stretch," I instruct as I put a pile of cash down on the table.

He pulls a card from a wooden dealer and shakes his head. "Winner. Congratulations, would you care to go double or nothing and really test your luck in front of the lady?" He propositions as he points to Penelope.

"Would you?" I say as I point to a hole in the wall in the back of the saloon. I give a quick tug on my zipper to really let him know I'm down for some action.

"Have a nice evening, sir," he says as he tips his hat and avoids eye contact.

I pick up my cash and walk back over to Penelope and hold it up, smiling. She shakes her head in amazement. I whistle to the keep for two more shots of whiskey.

"That's incredible. I can't believe that just happened. No one ever wins at those games," she says.

"I know. Plus, they love it when you win one hand and just walk away," I say as we share a laugh.

"So now what?" She asks coyly.

"Barkeep, your best champagne," I yell out as I throw a wad of cash at him.

The bartender returns and pops the cork on a bottle of champagne, and we begin to get loose. With all this extra bread and my new job starting in the morning I decided, why not treat myself? Let's go big.

After finishing off the champagne, I knew I had made a fatal mistake by drinking whiskey beforehand. Whiskey and champers makes me go fucking BOGO. I took the empty bottle of champs and smashed it against the wall, then pissed all over the piano player in the bar. Relax. I paid him forty bucks to do it. He didn't seem to mind. Forty dollars was a lot of money to people back then, and I should know, because I had to pay him to do it again later on that night. That's probably the most money he's ever seen in that joint.

Penelope could hold her own surprisingly. She was trashed, but she wasn't like "hobo trashed." It was the kind of drunk where you just gave zero fucks. With that much money, we could roll through town, fuck shit up, and just huck a pile of money in people's faces without repercussion. It was just like the old days.

We hit all the saloons, ate some squirrel di afterward, made fun of homeless people, fun shit. I saw a cat walking down the street with a missing eye, so I went into the jeweler, bought a diamond, and shoved that fucker right in his socket. You know how many people that cat must have freaked out walking through town with a diamond eye? Goddamnit I was awesome tonight.

Before heading back to the hotel, I stop and pay that fucking piano player once more to let me piss on him for the third time. It's not like it was a fetish of mine or anything, it was just the power of it. If you get a chance to piss on a stranger just because you're rich, I highly recommend it.

The hotel turned out to be really fucking nice too. We told the dude at the front desk that we were separated twins who had never had sex before, so he gave us the "honeymoon suite". The only complaints about the place were that the walls were super thin, and honestly, those complaints came from other people staying on the same floor as us.

This one guy kept screaming over and over, "THE WALLS ARE SUPER THIN! PLEASE STOP HAVING SEX!"

Based on her petite frame, I thought he meant her vagina walls, so obviously I didn't stop. The night turned blurry once the candle went out in our room. I literally couldn't see anything. I do remember her saying how strong and brave I was. Scratch that. I actually said that aloud to myself at some point during our coitis. Either way, it's a completely true statement and I deserved to hear it no matter who's mouth it came out of.

The following morning, I awaken to the screams, "GET HIM! GET HIM! GET HIM!"

The sunlight destroyed my retinas as if I had gotten Lasik surgery with my eyes closed. Fuck it burned. I stand up buck-naked and walk over to the window to see where the screaming is coming from. I pull it open and see five Mexicans chasing a cat into an alley.

"Get the fucking diamond!" one of them screams.

"Shut the fuck up down there," I yell down with a hoarse voice.

I don't even complete the sentence before heaving last night's drinkfest onto some innocent bystanders passing by. Luckily, one of the women I was puking on was holding up one of those bullshit "sun umbrellas", and most the sick just bounced off her *ella ella* on to the shoes of her husband. He looks up at me pissed as hell.

"Get a fucking job, loser!" he yells.

"I have a job you fucking ho—

Ralph Macchio.

The dude picks up the pace with his wife as they dodge round two. The good news is, I'm fairly certain there's nothing left inside of me and my hangover is clearing. The bad news is; my asshole really hurts. I stand by the window confused, trying to piece together the night. Was it the squirrel di? Did I allow myself to get pegged? What the fuck happened?

I look down at my cock and see a small gold chain tied around it. I tug on on it, which pulls my pocket watch out of my asshole. That explains the pain. I hold it up and wave it toward Penelope as she slowly rolls over and opens her eyes.

"You said you weren't that type of girl," I say surprised.

"Actually, you put the watch up your own ass," she says sheepishly.

"*Really?*" I ask confused.

"Yeah, you said something about wanting to get up early and the ticking would be a gentle reminder—

"Gentle reminder my ass—okay—now I know why I did that. Brilliant. What time is it?"

I flick the cover open on my timepiece which reads 11am. Shit. I'm five hours late for work. I get dressed as fast as possible and wash the shit off my watch in a water bowl on the dresser. Obviously, I couldn't help but smile, because it reminded me of my mining days and how I was headed back to work with Samantha. I turn back toward Penelope.

"I'm headed to work, but I'll stop at the front desk and let them know we're staying for awhile. I'll also ask for some fresh water," I say as I point to the bowl.

"I want to come with you," Penelope says.

"It's pretty rough out there and it's going to be boring as shit. Here's some cash to go shopping," I say as I throw some money down on the bed. "We'll grab dinner some place nice tonight when I get home."

"Okay," she says with a smile.

As I go to open the door, I find a note underneath it that contained only one sentence in all capital letters, "THE WALLS WERE TOO FUCKING THIN, AND I COULDN'T TAKE IT." That's strange. I turn the doorknob, but it doesn't budge. The next time I tug even harder and the door finally cracks open. After a few more pulls, it opens about three feet. I look down and see a man tied to the doorknob by what appears to be his own belt. He was dead. Oh well, if you can't take my fucking, you don't deserve to be alive in this world anyway.

Penelope stares at the man's lifeless body that is now pulled halfway into our room. Her eyes widen in horror. I pick up the note and jam it into my pocket, not wanting to freak her out that people could hear us.

"Strangle-bation. Some people take it to razor's edge in this world. I'll tell a bellhop to come get this body too. Have a good one," I say as I tip my hat before heading out.

I carefully step over the body and take a light jog down the stairs to the front desk. The clerk looks up at me and smiles.

"How did you sleep?" He asks.

"So good that I'll be staying indefinitely," I say.

"That's wonderful news!"

"Isn't it? Can you do me a solid and change out the water in my room, there's shit in it. Also, could you be a lamb and take the dead guy off the door that's still hanging there?"

His smile slowly fades and he mutters, "Um, sure."

"You're a peach," I say with a wink.

I head out front and hop on my steed, riding out toward the railroad tracks. It's a fairly short distance—about twenty minutes—so I feel pretty good about not being *that* late. Five and half hours isn't too bad considering what I did to my mind and body last night. When I pull up, I see Samantha smiling with what's left of his teeth. Goddamnit I missed that grin. I jump down and greet him.

"Somebody party too hard last night?" He asks.

"I woke up with my own pocket watch in my ass and a dead guy hanging from the doorknob. Does that answer your question?" I ask annoyed.

"It actually raises *more* questions," he says.

"Look Sam, we can tie two cans to a string and play telephone later, how's the track coming along today?"

He shrugs his shoulders, "Same as every day. We're Chinese, we really don't need anymore motivation than that."

"Valid point. How long is it going to take you guys to finish?"

"When we were working out west, we build forty miles then test it with a train," he says.

"Okay, how long does that take?"

"Five or six months, maybe more. Down here in Nebraska, when the tracks come in, we put them down as fast as we can. But we're only getting two miles worth of track at a time delivered to us," he says surveying the railroad.

"Why only two miles worth?" I ask.

"Don't know. It comes in sporadically. The man you killed say 'when it get here, it get here.' He don't tell us why. Some days we don't even work, just wait on tracks to come in," he says shrugging his shoulders.

"Jesus Christ, Samantha. How do we speed this up, both the conversation and this project?" I ask, twirling my index finger in a circle.

"Need more men, more steel."

"Who do I talk to about that?" I ask annoyed as shit.

"The man you killed, Mr. Navarro, his boss. His name Leland Stanford. He's out of California," Sam says as he really overemphasizes the words.

"I know that fat fuck. He used to be a gold merchant out in Michigan City. I sold to him a few times back in the day. How the hell did he get into this?"

"He used all his gold money to invest in wailwoads. He the richest man in California now," Sam says with an arched eyebrow, knowing that would sting.

"Alright. I'm going to travel back and have a chat with him, try and get you some more men. I guess I can finally bury Daniel while I'm there. Can you lead your guys here while I'm gone?"

"No problem, you've been here less than a day. I'll work day and night, never taking a break like always boss. If there's one thing I can do, it's relentless manual labor," he says with a huge smile.

"I knew I could count on you. See you soon," I say as I slap him on the back.

He folds like a wet accordion after that back slap, as I casually ride off. I can't help but think of how Leland fucking Stanford got rich enough to run a railroad company. To put who this man is into context, think of that fat kid on *Pawn Stars*, but all grown up. Yeah, fucking *Chumlee*.

Leland Stanford would literally sit and barter you to death over chunks of gold, hemming and hawing over how much he could sell them for in the open marketplace and then explain to you—in great detail—every single sexual position he was getting fucked in on the deal. It was a goddamn nightmare dealing with him, so I quit using him after three or four deals. I just couldn't put up with the bullshit of pretending to care about what he was saying anymore.

If that guy dickered like that over gold specks, imagine what he must be like to deal with on a fucking railroad? Just thinking about it was enough for me to decide that I should get drunk before going back to the hotel. I also probably deserve some head from a prosty. Just saying. My dick isn't going to suck itself. The only "me too" that occurred back then was when your buddy walked out of a prostitute's bedroom saying, "I only paid twenty."

#metoo

Chapter 11

I GRIEVE REAL FUCKING HARD

I'm not real fucking sure what happened to me last night, but waking up in a wheel barrow out front of my hotel to a cat with a diamond for an eye licking my face is pretty much what I expected. There's a nip in the air as winter was setting in and my pants were frosted over. I get up and hear a cracking noise, like icicles falling off a roof. Shit. I look down and realize that I pissed myself in the night and my fucking jeans are frozen solid. Hell of a way to start the day.

I walk in and greet the hotel clerk, who is not so chipper this morning. "I have some bad news. Looks like I won't be *staying here indefinitely.* Turns out I have to go out of town for business, so I'll be checking out today," I say.

His frown turns upside down faster than a fucking *Lionel Playworld.* "Thank God. We've lost so much business in the last forty-eight hours because of you, I didn't know if we'd survive the winter! Hallelujah!"

He reaches underneath the desk, pulls up a bottle of tequila, and begins chugging the entire thing down. I let him have his moment as I walk up the stairs, taking my jeans off in the process. You knew I was leaving these fucking things in the stairwell. There wasn't a goddamn prayer that they'd be making the journey out west. Penelope looks at me in shock as I open the door to the room half nude with my cowboy boots slung over my shoulder.

"Where have you been?" She asks in a worried tone.

"Probably every bar in this town. Would you mind drawing me a hot bath? We have to leave for California today."

"Really? Why?"

"Well, I pissed myself last night," I say in a hushed tone.

"No, I mean why are we going to California today?" She asks.

"Business. While we're there, I'm going to bury Daniel. We should probably be respectful and not bone until after he's in the ground, okay?" I ask her seriously.

Penelope shakes her head profusely, "Of course. Yeah, that's only right." She quickly starts to fan her face with both hands.

"Did you just get your nails done?" I ask.

"No, I'm sorry—this is a lot for me to take in right now. The actual prospect of burying Daniel didn't really hit me until this very moment," she says.

"If it makes you feel any better, the actual prospect of me waking up in a frozen pair of jeans that I pissed in, blacked out in a wheel barrow didn't hit me until it actually happened today too," I say nodding solemnly.

"That actually doesn't help," she says quickly.

"You're welcome. Now how about that bath? I'm feeling very vulnerable right now and I need to collect my thoughts in the claw foot."

She nods as I skin off and take a seat in the bath. I look out the window as she pours warm water over me and see snow begin to fall. It will be nice to get the fuck out of here and head back to the warm weather of California. The Nebraska Territory—actually the entire Midwest—is a strange climate. Very gray. You don't really see the sun that often and that shit wears on you.

Usually, I take my time and enjoy a good cock soak in the tub for a couple hours, but not today. I was so ready to bounce, so I didn't even ask for an HJ. As soon as I cleaned the piss off me, we packed up and left. On the way out I flipped the keys back to to the clerk, who snatched them out of the air and smiled.

"You guys leaving?"

"Yup. Have a good one," I say as I hand him some cash.

"Thank Christ!" he screams as he pulls out a brand new bottle of tequila and proceeds to down that one too.

After every drop is gone, he removes his penis and balls from his pants and lays them up on the front desk. He begins bashing his junk over and over with the bottle until it smashes. Penelope looks on horrified as he falls over on the ground, losing all consciousness.

"Wow. He really wanted us to leave," she says in a horrified whisper.

I shrug my shoulders. "Used to it. I can't wait to see the look on his face when we come back in a few months. He's going to shit in a canteen bottle. Come on."

As I grab her hand and head out the door, the chilly air decks us square in the face, as the snow flurries continue to fall. I pack up the carriage and safely put Penelope inside so she doesn't freeze to death. It's colder than a dog's dick in a copper thimble out here. I hop on my steed and ride west as fast as I can to beat the weather.

Unlike the journey to Nebraska, the trip out west was mostly uneventful. The hardest thing was trying to keep my penis out of Penelope on the colder nights. Once we hit Nevada, the weather started to warm up and I was back in my element. When I say "back in my element", I mean there was some fuck shacks in Nevada. During a couple of our stays in these shanty towns that we hit up for food and water, I'd sneak off to get tugged out just to try and maintain a respectable level of sanity. A man of my sexual prowess needed a strong bi-weekly release at a minimum, or I'd just start killing innocent people for no reason. I'm not kidding either.

I'll rewind to when we passed through Salt Lake City, Utah. It was fucking freezing and the snow was hellacious. There wasn't one goddamn fuck shack in that entire state, which meant there was no where to get off. Penelope had excused herself to use an outhouse in town, and a few homeless people walked up to me begging for money and food. I couldn't take their grimy fucking attitude, much less the fact that there wasn't a woman in the bunch, so I pulled out my six shooter and blew them all away. Dead. *Gandhi.*

When Penelope finished up her biz in the outhouse, she walked out and saw the homeless dudes dead in the snow and shrieked in dismay. I made up a story about how I dozed off and was awakened by four dirty as shit dudes trying to gang bang my horse while I was still on it. She seemed to buy it and didn't put up too much of a fuss, so fuck it. I know the real reason obviously.

You can go ahead and take that moral compass you just pulled out of your pocket and stuff it up your ass. It's not like those filthy fucks were going to go on and revolutionize the world like I was, so fuck'em. I probably did society a favor.

When we finally hit Coloma, California, memories came flooding back in like Katrina. The main street that used to be bustling with excitement and possibility was gone however. It was now relegated to a fucking ghost town. A lone tumble weed rolled slowly in front of my steed, then it appeared to just give up, breaking apart in front of us real fucking sad like. Jesus. Even a fucking tumble weed didn't even want to live anymore here.

The whore house and opium den I built was reduced to busted up doors and loose wood. If I would have breathed on it, that shit probably would have collapsed. There wasn't one single soul up in this motherfucker. I know what you're thinking, "Saint James Street James, wasn't it *your* drugs that destroyed the town?" The answer is no. They didn't.

The truth of the matter is, back then, when these mining towns ran out of gold—people got the fuck out of there. If there was no money to be made, there was no reason to be there anymore. Drugs were the defining measuring stick of how prosperous a town actually was then. If people were getting gacked out of their minds, that means they had money to spend and wanted to fucking party. No more money, no more party.

That's why these ghost towns popped up all over the Wild West like old Myspace profiles with Daft Punk's *Around The*

World still blaring. No one ever returned to clean them up, so they just left them. Don't believe me? Pop on over to your old Myspace page and enjoy your old pics of you with the *Blue Man Group* in Vegas circa 01'.

Riding up to where my house used to be, I halted my steed and jumped down. It was almost exactly as it was when I left, nothing but a pile of ashes. Penelope exited her carriage and walked over beside me, taking it in.

"Oh my God. It's totally fucking Mexico," she said softly.

"Yeah, shit was crazy. Did Daniel tell you about my dead son of the same name?" I ask, staring at the sun reflecting off the head of his golden statue.

Penelope looks at me and nods. "Yes. He spoke fondly of him."

"That was Daniel's favorite little brother. He was dipped in scalding hot gold and killed, somehow making for the perfect statue," I say as I point to Totally Fucking Mexico's solid gold body.

She looks down. "I'm sorry for your loss. Daniel actually didn't tell me how he died. He just said his brothers were all killed in a house fire and that was about it."

"Nothing about his dead human trophy brother, huh? Weird. Well, we all grieve in different ways I guess," I say as I kick some of the ashes really hard.

"Yeah," she says in an odd manor, probably thinking back to the night we first boned.

Up by the top of the hill where Totally Fucking Mexico stood, I noticed some headstones. That doesn't seem like something I would do, but I was on a lot of opium back then, so anything is possible I guess. As I walked up the hill, I could see the name "Rouretta" chiseled into the first headstone. Fucking Samantha. I couldn't help but smile at his complete Asian-ness.

The fact that he had taken the time to make headstones for each of the kids and Louretta, perfectly aligned next to Totally Fucking Mexico's statue, meant a lot. I could finally return Daniel home to his family once and for all. I motioned for Penelope to come up and join me.

"This is where he will be laid to rest," I say to her.

She squints trying to make sense out of the names on the headstones. "Who is Bwurbwan?"

"That's my other son, Bourbon Street James. Asian spelling. Fucking Samantha Davis, man."

She nods understanding. "Is there any friends or neighbors that you'd like to invite to the burial?"

"No, I had one Mexican friend who pretended to be Indian, but his bar was gone on main street. My only neighbors were gimpy-ass Ron and his wife Sheila—

I stopped myself mid-sentence as I peered down the hill to their house, which still appeared to be intact. I wonder if they still lived there even though the town was dead? I wonder how Sheila looks after six more years of aging? I wonder if I could get Ron to dig the grave for me? Digging a grave is legit hard as fuck. People don't understand. It's a fucking toll.

I turn toward Penelope, "Hang here. I'll see if the neighbors are still in town," I say as I hand her one of my pistols.

"That would be nice if they were," she says.

"You haven't met Ron. Being around that guy is like someone dropping a hot turd in your lap while wearing white linen pants. He fucking sucks at life."

Penelope seems taken aback. "That is a graphic image."

"You're lucky I didn't tell you about the time I shot his dick off. Anywho, I'll unhook the carriage and bring Daniel's casket up, then ride down and see if they are there. If you want to get started on that grave dig, you're obviously welcome to it."

"You're not serious?" She asks in a harsh tone.

"No, I was pulling your tit on that one. It's funny, you see women marching for equal opportunity and wanting to vote, but when it really comes down to it—

"Go see if the neighbors are home," she says very pointedly.

"Got it. By the way, if you're hungry, watch out picking berries. They might be old opium seeds. I used to be a drug dealer and I grew all over this whole area. If you find any poppy seeds left, it would mean the world to me if I could smoke them. Well, I'm off," I say as I tip my hat.

I chuck up a deuce sign and mosey on down the hill toward the carriage. After I unhook it from my steed, I pull a shovel out of the back of it and toss it toward the hill before I get back on my horse. She laughs, or whatever the opposite of that is.

"Just in case!" I yell out as I ride off.

I didn't look back, but I'm sure she enjoyed that line. Riding down to Ron's house along the river, I forgot how much I missed this place. The landscape is actually pretty beautiful. So much so, I take off my shirt so I can arrive at Sheila and Ron's house with a nice oiled lather just to let them know I still got it. I even give my penis two strokes to try and grab an extra flaccid inch. Needed to be done.

When I arrive, I look around the property and see signs of a bullshit vegetable garden out back that appears to be fresh. Son of a bitch, are they still here? Only one way to find out. I kick open the door, ripping it from it's hinges and draw my remaining pistol.

"IS ANYBODY FUCKING IN HERE???" I yell out in an angry black man's voice for emphasis.

A woman screams and drops freshly folded clothes on the ground and scurries behind a beam. "Wait, Saint James? Is that you?"

Sheila carefully steps out from behind the beam and smiles.

"Sheila?" I say as I squint a little.

"Yes, it's me. Do you not recognize me?" she says with a laugh.

"Sorry, yes, of course I recognize you. You just obviously just look older," I say as I help myself to an apple from the kitchen table.

"We're the same age," she says matter of factly.

"Yeah, but I'm a man, and I'm rich—so I've obviously beat the aging process altogether," I say between bites of the apple.

"What are you doing back in town?" She asks.

"Funeral. Daniel died. It's a difficult thing to have to bury your last remaining son," I say as I throw the apple on the floor.

"Well, you still have one son left," she says sweetly.

I look at her in shock. "What? Who?"

"Ours," she says as she points to a portrait on the wall of a kid who looks exactly like me. He's grown so much older than the last time I saw him.

"Oh shit. I forgot about that fucker. Isn't Ron looking after him?" I ask annoyed she even brought him up.

"Yes, he was... before he passed," she says looking down.

213

"Ron's dead? How?" I ask without trying to laugh.

"He got pretty horrible gangrene after you shot his penis off. The reattachment didn't go as hoped. I told him not to use those Mexicans in the back of a wagon behind the butcher shop, but he didn't listen."

"Classic Ron," I say with a chuckle.

"Yeah. He was a fighter though, he hung on for about four months," she says thinking back.

"Christ, that's a long time," I answer in disgust.

Sheila shakes her head. "I know. He even taped a carrot to where his penis was and hopped out of bed one day and said he was fine, but we all knew," she says tearing up.

"Ron was never subtle about the art of deceit. My condolences. So you live here alone now?" I ask.

"No, my son Saint James Street James Junior still lives with me."

"I can't believe you named him after me while you were still married to Ron."

"He looks exactly like you. It was only right," she smiles.

"I'm sure Ron appreciated the gesture. Is your son here? It would mean the world to me if I could see him," I say as I peer around the living room.

"Really?" She asks, genuinely touched.

"Yeah, I mean if I can see him before he spots me, then I can dip out and avoid an awkward conversation."

"Oh. Well, he's gone hunting for the night. He'll be back in the morning. After the mines went dry and all the businesses left, he's been helping me out by gathering food and supplies," she says earnestly.

"Why didn't you guys just move?" I ask.

Sheila bites her lip, holding back tears. "I was hoping you'd come back Saint James."

She moves closer to me and the sunshine coming in from the kitchen illuminates her face. Damnit, she has gotten *way* older looking, but her body is still banging. Motherfucker. You want to know what the original Crossfit is? Carrying fucking fruit and vegetables above your head in a wooden basket. Her legs and core were still amazing. I take a deep breath and lean into her, obviously knowing what I have to do.

"Sheila, I don't want to disappoint you but—

She puts her finger up to my lips. "Sssshhh. You won't. I'm not expecting anything from you."

"Sheila, it's not that. This light is really harsh on you. Would you mind?" I ask as I point to a burlap potato sack on the ground by the kitchen table.

"You want me to wear that on my head?"

"Would you be so kind? Sorry. I just want to be able to get off and enjoy this," I shrug.

"Say no more. I understand," she quietly nods.

"Thanks doll baby stroller."

She slowly starts to take off her clothes, revealing her vegetable WOD* body. It's as majestic as I remember. Sheila smiles, knowing it too. I take off my boots, because I'm not married now, and lay my jeans over a chair perfectly as to not fuck up my crease. She leans in to kiss me, pulling me on top of her on the kitchen table, before I politely stop her.

"Sheila, we can't—

"Because this is the table you fucked me on in front of Ron?" She asks.

"I don't care about that. It's the bag, Sheila. You still haven't put it on," I say as I pick it up off the floor.

Sheila shakes her head, "Of course. I'm sorry. I just got caught up in the moment."

"Let me help you get caught up fully then," I say as I place the bag in her hand.

Sheila puts the bag over head like a drunken bank robber. It's ill fitting, but it does the trick. I rip open a mouth hole through the burlap for her to breath more easily out of. It is an

---

* WOD – Is the bullshit term they call Workout Of The Day in Crossfit. Back then, we just called it "living your fucking life".

unforgiving material. I then grab a white piece of chalk off the table and draw some X's for eyes, just so visually, I have my own reference for a focal point. It has always been a requirement of mine that some sort of eye contact, even if perceived, is a necessity. Call me old fashioned.

I pull her legs up over my shoulders, giving her the exact same experience from the last time I fucked her on her kitchen table. My only regret is that Ron isn't around to see it again. I briefly contemplate asking Sheila how far his grave is for a quick exhume, but ultimately decide against it because I'm inside of her, and I thought it would be rude. Manners are the cornerstone of our—I don't fucking know. Add something poignant to the end of that in your own mind, I'm banging a woman on her table.

The next two hours are the type of slow grinding sex I'm accustomed to doling out. It's just as important for me to give her the same performance as I gave her last time, not only for my own personal pride, but also for the fact she has been waiting for this dick for years. It's the same reason Michael Jordan always wore a suit out in public, he knew this might be the only time you ever get to see him, so he wanted to leave you with that one lasting memory. The same can be said about me in the bedroom.

When I'm positive I have repeated my excellence, I decide it's time for me to climax. Right as I'm about to explode, Shelia's son walks through the front door holding a dead chicken by the neck. I turn, startled, and my penis slips out of her vagina and I ejaculate all over the bag covering her face. He looks at me in horror.

"Dad?"

I'm at a loss for words. I shrug my shoulders and blurt out the first thing that comes to mind when an illegitimate father sees his son for the first time in years, "Bring it in."

He drops a carrot he was holding in his other hand on the floor and walks over to me and gives me a big hug. I honestly didn't think he would because I had just pulled out, but a father/son bond is strange sometimes. Sheila takes the bag off her head and smiles, welling up once again.

"This is nice, isn't it?" she says through her tears.

Fuck no it isn't, but what am I supposed to say in this sitch? Shelia glances down at the carrot on the floor and I can tell the irony is not lost on her. I fucking hope Ron is watching down on this shit. He deserves to see this moment. When Saint James Street James Junior finally breaks the hug, I look him and slap him on the shoulder.

"Who's ready for a funeral?" I ask.

Saint James Street James Junior stares at us in confusion. "Honey, can you give us a minute?"

"Sure mom," he says before he walks outside.

Sheila tosses the burlap bag on the ground and we begin to put our clothes on as I try not to look at her as I zip up. "How old is your boy? Twenty-seven?"

"No, he's twelve," she says.

"Ah, that's a fun age isn't it? Only one of mine made it past that age, but I'm told it's great."

"Yeah. He's an amazing kid," she says with pride.

"That's good to hear. He should have no problem digging a grave then. Anywho, I'm sure you guys will probably ride together, so I'm going to get the fuck out of here. You know where I live. See you soon."

"Hey Saint?" She asks in a super desperate voice, wanting me to turn around.

I exhale deeply and roll my eyes until they are completely crossed before turning around. "Yes?"

"This was nice. I'm glad you came back," she says sincerely.

"Then you can prove it to me by bringing some food to the funeral. My house is burnt to shit and I'm fucking starving."

"Of course," she nods understandingly.

On my way out, I spot an old saddlebag with a few dynamite sticks peeking out of it. The name branded into the bag reads: **4 Prawn Ron.** I stop and do a double take.

"Shelia, what the fuck does four prawn Ron mean?" I ask.

"That's just a nickname he gave himself. Ron was a huge fan of shrimp cocktails," she says slightly embarrassed.

"Of course he was. I'm taking this," I say.

"Please do. Get it the fuck out of here," she replies.

I sling the saddlebag over my shoulder, walk out, and mount my steed with the old "two hand on the ass leap" and take off as fast as possible. The two handed ass mount is for when you don't want to look back when you're leaving. It's ideal for a sitch like this.

As I ride off, I find it strangely comforting that even in death, Ron is still embarrassing to his wife. Also, it's important to note that you can't give yourself a nickname. That shit has been a golden rule since humans could fucking communicate to each other back in caves. You especially shouldn't give yourself the nickname of an appetizer. Jesus man.

On the way back to the burnt remains of my house, I decided to have myself a good old fashioned dynamite montage. Ron had a tiny bottle of Hennessy in his bag like a bitch, but of course I drank it. Fuck that guy. You would have figured I could let go of my hatred, but this dude just kept sucking.

One by one, I lob sticks of dynamite into the air at random objects, and I feel free. You know that look on white girls faces when they throw a pile of leaves in the air in October and have their friend shoot it in slo-mo so they can hashtag it "Fall" on

Snapchat? That's the look I had when I was chucking boomsticks. Pure elation.

When I finally return back to my property, Penelope is rummaging through the ashes, placing tiny objects into her dress that she has slightly flipped up. The dress is raised high enough that I can see her beautiful ass cheeks, which resemble two peaches escaping a wooden crate stamped "Grown In Georgia". I hop off my steed and whistle, letting him know to hydrate down at the river.

"What are you doing?" I ask.

She turns with a look of confusion on her face. "You asked me to look for poppy seeds. Are these them?"

She unfolds her dress slightly revealing a handful of that sweet Chinese molasses. That Dream Stickiness. The Midnight Oil. God's Medicine. The two-legged donkey kick. I thought I was going to cry. Sometimes there's so much beauty in this world I can't take it, some asshole once said in a movie that I hated. I walk over to her and she pours them out into my hand, so I could check the authenticity. They were still good.

"Thank you so much. This means more to me than you'll ever know," I say genuinely touched.

"You're welcome. What are you going to do with them?" She asks.

"I'm going to smoke that shit. On a day as difficult as this one, I should probably be well medicated. I'm going to grab my pipe from my steed down by the river," I say as I tip my hat.

"Shouldn't you start digging the grave?" She asks.

"No, I knocked up a neighbor years ago, so my illegitimate child who looks exactly like me is going to do that. His mom will be coming as well. Please forgive her age," I say as I walk off.

After getting completely blasted off opium down by the river, followed by several hours of watching St. James St. James Jr. dig a grave, we finally held a small service with just the four of us. Shelia consoled Penelope while I gave a sermon. It was unseasonably hot that day, and I was sweating my ass off. It caused the opium to kick in harder than normal, considering I hadn't done it in awhile. When I finish, everyone politely claps.

I walk over to console Penelope who is weeping. "How did I do? I hope I memorialized Daniel properly."

"Oh, you didn't talk about Daniel at all. You spent the full hour talking about soil fertility recommendations for Christmas trees," she says between tears.

"Well, grief sometimes takes us down a long dusty road full of emotions and wonderment," I say, realizing I'm still seeing tracers.

Shelia approaches me gingerly. "That was, um, an interesting sermon you delivered for your son. He would have been proud?" She asks as if it were a question.

"Indeed he would be. He loved Christmas very much," I say not knowing if that's true.

"That's lovely. I made the food you requested. Due to the heat, and you not having a free standing structure on your land, I figured it might be more pleasant if we ate at our house," Sheila says shrugging her shoulders.

I pull Shelia aside from the other two. "Is this some kind of game where you get off serving food to everyone on the table we fucked on? What is your damage Sheila?"

"What? No! I just—thought it would be a nice retreat from the heat. I have chairs for everyone and—

"I'm kidding. That's a lovely gesture, thank you Sheila. Why don't you take everyone down to your house and I'll meet you there? I want to bury my son alone please. Penelope, you can take my horse," I call out to her.

"What about you? I can wait," she says.

"No. I need to do this by myself."

Penelope nods, as the three of them start heading over to the horses. I pick up the shovel and slowly begin throwing dirt on top of the grave. I feel like he's died so many times, which of course, he has. Something inside of me though keeps thinking he'll pop up alive. Maybe that's why I can't bring myself to pick up the pace.

"Get up Daniel," I keep saying aloud.

Over the course of the next two hours, I must have said that phrase a hundred times. Alas, he did not get up. It was time to finally say goodbye. I put the shovel down and grab my pipe from my saddlebag that Penelope left, before sitting down with him once more.

I pack another bowl full of opium and take a deep pull, exhaling all over his headstone, hoping his body might catch some vapors. As I sit here, I think back to the first time I let him smoke the white lady inside of my old whorehouse where I paid for him to lose his virginity. He was so nervous that he was trembling. I begin to tremble as well, knowing that I'm probably near an overdose—and in this extreme heat—I could die on his grave, so I decide to stop smoking. Instead, I lie the beautiful Chinese piece on top of the dirt, leaving the ultimate tribute a father could give his son; his prized opium pipe. RIP Daniel.

Grief stricken, I look over and see the portrait of Louretta peeking out of my bag. I walk over and grab it, then lick the back of it and stick it to her tombstone. I take a seat on top of the grass as I stare at Samantha's misspelling of her name. It's as if her portrait wants to say something to me.

"Talk to me Lou. I need you right now you dirty bitch," I whisper.

A gust of wind blows from behind, flipping the picture up and down slightly. The sun has just set and I see the bright full moon illuminating the sky. I look up to the big guy for a sign. He smiles at me and mouths the words, "Go for it. Nobody's watching."

I nod my head. That fucking moon knows me so well. As I stare at her picture, I feel an erection rising faster than Jesus on Easter, so I unzip my pants. I take my hands and dig out a decent size hole into the grass, before slowly inserting my penis into the ground. Never breaking eye contact with Louretta's nude portrait, I start to make love to her grave.

I'm not going to go into the entire graphic description of the next four hours, just know it ended in a beautiful climax of me giving my seed back to the earth. I also really want to point out that I was super fucked up, and in no way have I ever done something like this again in my life. In this moment, it just felt right. Isn't that what life is? Just a person wanting to feel right? *Exactly.* You answered your own question didn't you?

After I pull my dick out of the ground, I knelt and kissed Louretta's headstone. Before leaving the property, I also gave a fist bump to Totally Fucking Mexico's gold statue, and of course I took one last hit off the pipe on Daniel's grave since the weather had cooled off. I walk down to Shelia's house with the moon at my back, completely at peace having said a proper goodbye to my family.

I re-kick open the door that someone tried to repair at Sheila's house when I get there. I'm immediately greeted by Saint James Street James Jr. who asks, "Dad, why are your jeans all dirty?"

"I had someone I had to say goodbye to. Maybe you will too one day. Holy fucking shit this is a nice ass spread," I say looking at the food.

The kitchen table where I fucked Shelia on earlier has more food on it than Thanksgiving at Amy Schumer's house. Famished, I immediately sit down and start helping myself. I can feel Penelope staring daggers at me.

"Do you want to take a bath first?" She asks moderately disgusted.

I stop mid-bite and glare at her, "Why? It's not like I'm eating dinner off myself. How about you look inside *yourself* before looking at others. Judgment starts from within. Pocahontas said that."

Penelope shakes her head as I continue eating. I marvel over the fact how it never gets old stuffing food in your face while you're this high. It's fucking insanity how well certain drugs and food go together. Amazon should just sell them both as a package deal and cut out the middle man.

As we eat, I look around the table and realize how grateful I was to be around family on this day. By family, I mean my illegitimate kid and these two women that I've had sex with various times. I hadn't sat down and shared a meal at the dinner table with somewhat loved ones since I lived up the road. It really is like they say, a burnt down home is where the heart is.

Chapter 12

I'LL GIVE YOU MY HAMMER

April 15th, 1865

I wake up the following morning to the scent of pancakes and a tingling sensation running through my body. When I open my eyes, I see Shelia on top of me wearing a pancake on her face with jagged eye holes cut out of it, connected to a piece of yarn tied around the back of her head. She covers my mouth and begins riding me slowly.

"I couldn't find the burlap sack, so I had to improvise," she says muffled through the pancake.

"Goddamnit Shelia, I gotta go to Sacramento today. I don't have time to give you all I got—

"I know. I'll make it quick. I didn't know if you were ever coming back, so *this* happened," she whistles as she waves her hand in front of her face indicating the pancake mask.

I exhale deeply, "Fine. We climax together on the the count of 127. It's a prime number that I feel comfortable with, okay?"

She nods her head and begins quietly counting aloud. The prime number thing was bullshit by the way. It just sounded good at the time, and she seemed into it, so fuck it. It's something that sticks with people just long enough that they'll start to incorporate it into their daily lives as some sort of deep meaning, and that's the type of shit I get off on. So on the count of 127, we both came. As she slowly climbs off of me and begins putting on her clothes, I motion to her—

"Do you mind?" I say as I point to her pancake.

"Not at all," she said somewhat surprised as she pulls the yarn off the mask, handing it to me.

"Thanks," I say as I begin clean my junk off with it.

Look, I have a long journey ahead of me, and I for damn sure wasn't going to use my shirt as a catch rag. Shelia waves at me after she finishes dressing, before quietly creeping out of my room. I look over on the nightstand and see a picture of Ron, posing with his saggy holster and fake wig sewn into his skull back when he was trying to be me. I laugh to myself, then throw the pancake against it, perfectly sticking the landing. Nice way to buttfuck the day.

When I walk out, I was sprightlier than usual at this time of the morning. Shelia, Penelope, and SJSJ Jr. were seated at the kitchen table eating large stacks of pancakes. Shelia smiles as if she wasn't just riding my dick earlier with one of those flap jacks on her face. I always respected her for that. Not only could she play the game, but she knew the rules. That's rare for a woman so desperate for a man like me.

"We saved some pancakes for you, how did you sleep?" Penelope asks with a smile.

"Never butter," I say. Shelia almost chokes on her pancake at my shitty joke. I think she was in the middle of 127 chews.

Saint James Street James Jr. stops eating and looks up at me. "Mom said you're going to Sacramento today?"

"Yes. I have a meeting there this afternoon that I'm just showing up for unannounced," I say stuffing my mouth full of pancakes.

"Can I come with you Dad?" He asks yearning for a father figure that I'm definitely not.

"No. There's a lot of... bees down there," I say as I continue to eat.

He looks at me confused. "So, what does that mean exactly?"

"I don't fucking know. It's the name of the city's newspaper and it sounded better than me saying I DON'T FUCKING KNOW YOU BRO."

"Saint James Senior," Shelia interrupts, pleading with her eyes for me to be softer with him.

"I mean, I don't know anything about your skills. What your assets are. I can only go off the fact that Ron raised you, and that leads me to believe you're incompetent and gimpy like he was. No offense," I say holding up my hands.

"None taken," both he and Shelia answer simultaneously.

"I'd hate to see you get your damn near identical face blown off for hanging around an outlaw like me. That's all I'm trying to say."

SJSJ Jr. nods and takes it in before speaking up. "I'm a decent shot and I won't get in the way. Plus, we look exactly alike and I could be your body double in case things get too hot."

I slam my fork down on the table. "You're fucking twelve. I look young, but not *that* young."

He looks up at me with pleading eyes like Daniel used to do. "Please Pa?"

"I don't know," I say as I pick my fork back up.

"What about me?" Penelope asks.

I slam my fork back down again. "Goddamnit! What's with the all fucking questions? I would pay a king's ransom to stuff another flapjack in my mouth right now in silence."

"Sorry," Penelope says retreating.

"With the funeral being over and whatnot, do you want to go home? You must have family back east right?" I ask Penelope.

She shakes her head softly, "No. They all died in a house fire as well. My little sister knocked over her night light, which was literally a lit lantern of fire. Everyone perished."

"Shit. Look, it makes sense. Houses are made with all wood; the only way we can see is with fire. What are the chances that both us lost our families in house fires? Actually, now that I'm saying it out loud, the chances are pretty high," I say as I mentally calculate the numbers.

"She can stay with me while you boys go? It'll be good to spend some quality time with Saint James Street James Junior alone. I can help Penelope get some supplies together for wherever you're headed to next," Sheila says.

I don't like any of this bullshit, but I'm kind of stuck at this moment. It's not like I can roll up to a meeting with a woman that isn't there for a bukkake sesh. I also don't want to hang out with the fucking kid that I don't know. Ultimately, I don't know what I'm getting into out there, and I might need another shooter. The ride is only a couple hours, so at least I'll be back by nightfall. I turn to the kid and nod.

"Fine. Let's go kid. Sheila, you stay here," I say resigned to the fact.

I stuff one last jack in mouth and light up a heater as I head out the front door with my doppelganger in tow. He's got a decent steed, obviously not the caliber of mine, but it'll do. I pull off a Street Howitzer attached to my saddle and throw it to him.

"You handy with the steel?" I ask.

"I'm a good shot," he says nervously.

"Well, the best thing about the Howitzer is that you don't have to be. Point and shoot, and you're bound to take off a body part of someone."

"Got it," he nods eagerly.

His desire to please reminds me of Daniel when he was that age. "Good. We ride in silence the whole way there. If you want to talk to me, we can pull our horses over and braid each other's pubes like ladies if you really feel the need to chat. *Comprende?*"

He nods, "No problem."

"Good. Let's ride out," I say as I snap the reigns on my steed.

The ride to Sacramento was relatively quick and every bit as drab as it sounds. Current day Sacramento is a shithole place to live that I wouldn't wish on anyone, imagine how it was back in the 1860's? Yup, that's exactly the image you were picturing.

Leland's office was situated on the downtown main street with a railroad car out front. Kind of an obvious choice for the "look who owns a railroad company" vibe, but whatever. He might as well put out a jar full of rulers so we can measure our dicks on the way in, since that's what he's going for. We hop down off our steeds, and I finally speak the first words to SJSJ Jr. I've said the entire way.

"Don't say anything when we get in the meeting. If he asks what you're doing here, I'll tell him you are a deaf mute who was raped by a pack of stray mules as a child when we were on a Grand Canyon expedition. Okay?"

"Okay," he says confused.

"Also, when we enter the room, pick a spot on the wall three inches above his forehead and just stare at it as hard as you can without blinking. I want you to really sell your disabilities."

He nods, trying to make sense of it, as we head into the office. When we walk in, we're greeted by a smokeshow of a secretary in her late twenties with blonde hair, huge tits, and glasses. She smiles warmly and looks up from her paperwork.

"Hello gentlemen, are you here to see Mr. Stanford today?" She asks politely.

"I am. My son had to accompany me at the last minute, so please forgive me," I say as I remove my hat.

"No problem at all." She reaches underneath the desk and pulls out a jar full of rulers and hands them to me. "If you wouldn't mind heading out back and giving me a measurement for Mr. Stanford, that would be great."

What the fuck did I tell you? Railroad car out front, we're measuring dicks. I look at her and unzip my pants, dropping the full Continental breakfast on her desk. She looks at my cock in disbelief like when the screen cut to black during the finale of *The Sopranos*.

"My eyesight ain't so good. Would you mind?" I ask with pride.

"Oh my," she gasps, staring at my large penis.

She scribbles down a "9" on a piece of paper and looks up at Saint James Junior, "You ready honey?"

"Um, my son lost his pecker in a freak wagon wheel accident, so he doesn't have one," I say as I motion to his groin area.

"Oh, I'm so sorry," she says, quickly putting the rulers away.

Saint James Street James Junior stares at the wall and licks his lips, playing it up. It's nice that he went along with it. I really didn't need to double dick on a stranger's desk with my 12-year-old son today, so he scored some points by recognizing that.

The secretary walks us back into Mr. Stanford's office, and hands him the results of my measurement. This tubby fucker looks the same as I remember him, except fatter and older. He's squeezed into a tweed suit with a vest that looks like it would pop open if he ate an olive. Looking down at the results, he shakes his head and squints, before removing his glasses altogether. With a surprised facial expression, he looks up at me, and I beat him to the question.

"It's a nine, holmes. Flaccid," I say with a wink.

"What? That can't be?" He asks, looking at his secretary.

"I'll drop this hammer like a test your strength game at the state fair if you'd like?" I ask, challenging him.

"It's real. I can *definitely* confirm it," the secretary says, trying to conceal her excitement.

He waves her off. "That'll be all Ms. Rhodes," he says hastily.

"If you need anything else, a re-measurement perhaps, I'm more than happy to—

"Nope. We're all good," he says.

She winks at me and taps a ruler in her hand as she exits. Mr. Stanford looks back down at the paper, and then curiously at the boy. "This one lost his dick in a wagon wheel accident it says? In all my years, I don't believe I've ever heard of something like that."

"There was a lot of blood. I'm not even sure what happened to the bag of cats after that. His first father was into some real strange shit. Now he's pretty much catatonic. No pun intended," I say with a serious demeanor.

He looks up at Saint James Street James Junior who stares just above his forehead at the back wall as I instructed. "Well, take a seat. What the fuck can I do for you today?"

I sit down in the chair in front of him and remove my cowboy hat. "I work for President Abraham Lincoln who has assigned me to help build the Transcontinental Railroad from Omaha moving west, and I'd like to speed this thing up—

He waves his hands in front of face stopping me. "You mean you *worked* for him."

I look up at him bewildered. "What do you mean *worked*? I still do."

"Not anymore. You didn't hear?" He asks.

"Hear what motherfucker?" I say as I'm getting angry at him for constantly cutting me off.

He picks up a folded newspaper off the desk and throws it at me, hitting me square in the chest. "He's dead."

"What? That can't be," I say, refusing to entertain the notion.

I open the newspaper and read the headline: **President Lincoln Assassinated.** Goddamnit. I stare at the paper in anger, not wanting to believe it. In all sincerity, I am legitimately sad inside at this moment. Linc did more than most men have done for me in my life and he really was a cool motherfucker.

"If you're going to cry, go outside. I have important things to do today," Mr. Stanford interrupts.

I snap out of my rage, and return a glare toward him that could have melted his fucking face off. "I have things to do today as well, *Leland*. And you are incorrect, I *still* work for President Lincoln, as the work on the railroad he requested is not complete. I'm going to see that through no matter what."

"Oh yeah? Who is going to pay you now? The government? The incoming president? I hope your friends with him too. Otherwise you are shit out of luck," he chuckles.

"No sir, you are, if I leave this project. You'll have no one to personally deal with on the construction and connection from Omaha to here."

"Not so. I have my guy Mr. Navarro."

"Dead. I killed him. Try again," I say without blinking.

He tries to dismiss me. "Then I'll hire someone else."

I quick draw my pistol and blow the head off a mounted deer head behind him. Antlers shatter into the air, whizzing past his head. Now Mr. Stanford becomes startled.

"I'll fucking kill them too. Let me put this in simpler terms that you can understand. Everyone you send will either die by my hands, or by the trigger on my steel. If you want this railroad completed this century, you will let me do my fucking job and I'll see you for the final spike."

He sits back in his chair and pulls his hand through his beard, realizing he's stuck. Leland shakes his head and sighs. "What do you need?"

"I need supplies delivered faster to my men. Right now they are only getting two miles worth of track at a time and there's a lot of people sitting around waiting."

He shakes his head. "We can't send anymore than two miles at a time because of train robbers. Right now our Union Pacific track only runs so long. We send the tracks as far as the current railway runs, then our workers take them down to Omaha. Problem is, eight out of ten trains are getting robbed and they're either pulling the rails, or blocking them with rocks. The train itself either derails before we can get it to the crew, or it's delayed for an ungodly amount of time."

I laugh and shake my head, "So all you need is someone to prevent the robberies from happening?"

"Precisely. Otherwise this goddamn thing won't get built until 1900. I don't get paid until it's finished, so I want this done as quickly as possible too."

I kick my boots up on this desk and cross my feet. "If I can stop these robberies from happening, what will you pay me?"

Now he kicks his feet up on the table and leans back in his chair. He pulls out a cigar, lights it, and stares up at the ceiling Brando in *Godfather* style. Mr. Stanford exhales deeply.

"I'll give you two," he says stone-faced.

"Two hundred thousand? You got yourself a—

"Two *million* dollars."

I almost choke on my hand rolled cigarette. "Two million you say?"

"That's right. Ten percent of my contract," he says puffing on a cigar.

"Goddamn, you go from nickel and diming filthy fucking miners for gold to a twenty-million-dollar railroad deal? Fucking America man," I say with a laugh.

He holds his index finger up and pulls his legs down, leaning over the desk toward me in a serious manner. "It's all about the *if*. *If* this railroad gets completed, I get twenty million. *If* not, then I get nothing. You understand?"

"I understand," I say as I remove my boots from his desk and lean into him, shaking his hand. "Luckily killing is something I'm real good at."

"Okay—

"No, I don't think you understand. It's a sickness. There's not one single morning I don't wake up and think to myself, fuck, I hope I get to kill someone today. On the days when I don't get to light someone up, I'm almost depressed. Maybe that's why I turn to the bottle and whore so much. Shit, I've never said that out loud before. Actually, can I start right away? I could really go for icing someone down tonight."

He stares at me with his mouth agape, "Um, sure. My secretary will give you a map of where the routes start."

"I appreciate it," I say as I put my hat back on and exit, tugging the arm of Saint James Street James Junior.

I grab the maps on the way out and debate whether or not to bone the secretary in the back alley, but ultimately decide against it. I'm sure homeboy desperately wants to take a shot at her and I don't want to fuck up an unbelievable payday. Don't think that once the money is in hand I'm not putting every last inch inside of her though. That ass looks like a blast.

Once me and Junior mount our steeds, he finally breaks character and unretards. He looks over at me with a smile. I know he wants some affirmation, so I decide to throw him a compliment.

"You did good kid. I'm sure Ron never told you that, so enjoy this moment," I say.

"Actually, he told me that every day he was alive," Junior says.

"Yeah, but that doesn't mean shit coming from a man like him. When it comes from my mouth, it really resonates."

"Does this mean I can come with you on your delivery routes?" He asks.

I look deep into the distance yet again. One part of me is thinking about how useful he would be to me out there. He's only twelve. They other part of me is still thinking about the tits on that secretary and how I'm going to destroy that beaver once this is over. After twenty uninterrupted minutes of staring at the sky, I finally turn back to him.

"Yes. You can go, if your mom says so. It sounds like it's going to be dangerous out there, so if you get killed, at least it won't be me. We'll ride back to Sheila's in silence and head out in the morning if you're lucky," I say as I take off.

When we return home, Saint James Street James Junior immediately asks her if he can come with me. Of course she said "yes". Seeing as how I only managed to keep one of my kids alive past twelve years old, I wouldn't have let him come with me if I was her. Whatever. I'm not her fucking husband.

We all sit and enjoy one last fine meal together with Penelope and Shelia. Goddamn, Shelia can really fucking cook. I'm so full, I unzip my jeans and pull them down to my calves. You ever eat so much that your quads feel bloated? It happens to me all the time. So much so that I wish I could just eat all my meals pants-less, but people would freak the fuck out in restaurants, so I refrain. In front of somewhat family, I feel perfectly justified in my decision. Penelope leans over to me and squeezes my arm mid-meal.

"Saint James, can I talk to you on the porch for a few minutes?" She whispers.

"Sure," I say as I stand up and hop out the front door, not bothering to pull my pants up.

I sit down in an old rocking chair and reach down into my pockets and pull out yet another hand rolled heater to fire up. Smoking is so fun and that's why I've never quit. It's a nice night out and I'm glad I'm pant-less, the fresh airs feels great on my genitalia. I offer Penelope a smoke and she obliges.

"So, what the fuck do you want?" I ask non-lovingly.

"What is this?" She asks as she takes a deep inhale of her smoke.

"It's tobacco held together by paper, but I'm not sure which region it's grown in—

"No, I mean what is this thing between me and you? Do you want a relationship?"

"I'm no bread man, but that question had a lot of ginger in it. Are you asking me to be in a relationship with you Penelope?"

"Yes I—

"Because the answer is no. Sorry. I was taking a beat before delivering my answer as to not crush your dreams so fast. Now it sounds like I jumped your answer, which isn't the case," I say trying to clarify.

Penelope looks genuinely upset. "Okay. I get it. So, do you want me to leave when you guys take off in the morning?"

"Look Penelope, I don't know what to say. Relationship wise, I don't want to get married again. I had a wife an eight kids, and they're all dead. I don't want another eight kids to raise," I say as I take a drag.

"Who says we would have eight kids?" She asks slightly puzzled.

"God says that. My cock is a vessel that delivers babies throughout the land. I hardly ever pull out and my sperm is super strong. Eight is a minimum depending on long you stay alive. Also, if we did have a kid and you were married to my son, wouldn't that make me the grandfather to my own child essentially? I don't want to bring my third generation into this world by myself."

She slowly nods her head considering my very valid points. "So what do you want to do then?"

"Reverse cowgirl?" I ask with a shrug.

This solicits a nice laugh from her, breaking up the seriousness of this conversation. She looks over at me with a smile. "Be real with me."

"Look, you're a great bang and hang, so if you want to come with me and Saint James Street James Junior, I'd be happy to have you. You can ride the train back with me and if you see a nice city you'd like to relocate to, you can get off at any time. I obviously mean that both literally and sexually. At the very minimum, I'm sure we would have a fun time for what it's worth."

She takes another puff of her smoke and contemplates her future. "I think it would be a fun time."

"I think so too Penelope—

"Reverse cowgirl. Sorry, you didn't let me finish my sentence," she says with a smile.

"Nailed it," I say with a laugh.

"You might end up falling in love with me, you know that right?"

"This tree takes a lot of chops to fall hard, so I doubt it. Now how about that reverse cowgirl we talked about?"

Penelope puts her cigarette out with her boot as she stands up. She pulls her dress up and sits down on my now hard penis facing the river—perfect reverse cowgirl style. We slowly bone as the rocking chair moves back and forth on the porch. The moon winks at me, appreciative of me letting him watch. I wink back at him, knowing he needed to see this. It was a beautiful night.

Chapter 13

YOUR HAND IN... HOLY SHIT

The next morning, we said goodbye to Shelia after breakfast. She understood when I said she couldn't come due to her looks. I needed to sell us as a nice normal, extremely attractive family and she obviously didn't fit the brand I was trying to portray. I probably could have passed her off as my second wife in a Mormon marriage, but I didn't feel like dealing with that fucking baggage. She said something about keeping her son safe, but I wasn't paying attention. The railway was calling.

We venture back to Sacramento to catch the train heading east containing the supplies and new tracks. According to the map, the railway would take us through Nevada and stop somewhere shortly after we crossed the California border. It was hard to tell where the train tracks ended on the map, simply for the fact that they were being extended every day.

When we got to the makeshift train station, I put our steeds in an animal boxcar and took Penelope and Saint James Street James Junior to one of the passenger cars. As other people began to board the train, I instructed my fake family to sit with me in the middle of the car. This way we could blend in like any other family. I didn't want to announce who I was in case we did get into trouble. The element of surprise would be my only advantage.

"If anyone asks you guys who you are, just say we are the Gelson family from Bakersfield, California," I say just above a whisper. "Penelope, you are Greta Gelson, my wife of four years."

"What's my name, Dad?" Saint James Street James Junior asks.

"You are Nelson," I say.

He squints his eyes and looks at me with a sour face. "Wait, I'm Nelson Gelson? Doesn't that sound kind of suspicious?"

"No. It sounds like a name a father gives his son so he doesn't fucking forget it. You got me holmes?" I say sternly.

He nods his head and looks straight forward. "So what's your name going to be?" Penelope asks.

"Barbados," I reply.

"What? Why? That doesn't sound like a real name," she says, shaking her head.

"It sounds like a strong Viking name. Someone who is in charge of the family, but also knows how to have a good time. You will not question Barbados Gelson like this in front of strangers, you understand? You will both respect your husband and father."

"Okay, whatever," Penelope sighs.

"Now, we will all have a nice relaxing ride like a family. If anything happens, then obviously I'll kill everyone. Let's just enjoy riding the rails powered by nature's most environment friendly complex resource, coal."

With all the passengers now safely onboard, the train roars to life as plumes of thick dark smoke pour from the engine. I look around the car to see if I spot anyone suspicious. So far everyone seems like your standard fair, except for a balding gentleman in his late forties across from me who removes his shoes as the train starts to roll. What the shit?

"Pardon me, sir?" I question him in a harsh tone.

He looks over at me annoyed. "Yeah?"

"Is there a reason why you removed your shoes on this train car?" I ask.

"It's a long ride, and I want to relax," he says in an annoyed manner.

"Let me ask you something, does your house have the exact interior of this train?"

"No, why?"

"Cool, then that means this isn't your fucking home, so don't act like it. Put the muzzles back on those barking dogs before I make stumps out of those two saplings. If I wanted the smell of wet ham slapping me in face, I'd eat the ass out of a drowning pig," I say with aggression.

The man furrows his brow as a nervous heat fart overtakes him. A couple people cough behind him as he quickly puts back on his shoes. I was about to kill this motherfucker just for making me this uncomfortable in a small space like this. People who have no sense of shame like this deserve to die.

I pull my cowboy hat over my eyes and enjoy a delightful slumber as the locomotive rumbles across California. There's something so peaceful about sleeping on a train. Especially when the woman next to you has her hand on your cock. I didn't even bother to look up at her, it was just nice knowing it was there. Sometimes it really is the thought that counts.

As we head over Donner Pass in the Nevada mountains, I hear a loud train whistle being pulled multiple times, and I bolt upright. If someone is going to wake me up from a nice cock cup on a train, someone better be dead on those fucking tracks ahead. With the train slowing down, I stand up and poke my head out the window and see a large pile of rocks stacked up on the tracks. A group of about ten or so outlaws with bandanas covering their faces sit on their horses with guns drawn. Shit is about to go down.

I motion to Saint James Street James Junior to get ready as I pull my pistol. Before Junior can even make it to the aisle, one of the outlaws fires his six shooter into the dome of the train conductor up front. His lifeless body falls out of the car and hits the gravel. The passengers scream in horror, as women quickly cover their eyes. Damn. Homeboys are playing for fucking keeps.

I fire a shot out the window, capping one dude in the chest. He slumps down from his horse and hits the dirt. The rest of the outlaws quickly retreat a few paces while trying to figure out where the shot came from. Saint James Street James Junior moves in right behind me.

"I've got your back Dad. I'll do whatever you need," he says eagerly as he draws his gun.

"I know you will, son. Here's what I want you to do. Exit the train slowly from the right hand door, while I take the left. We'll just keep firing until we meet in the middle at the front of the train. I'll distract them with my voice. Got it?"

He nods and begins moving toward the right hand door, as I walk toward the left hand door. When I see him safely exit and creep around the side of the train, I stick my head out again on the opposite side of him. I motion for the passengers to be as quiet as possible.

"I don't think you boys know who you're sticking up on this train?" I call out to them.

"And who might that be? Why don't you enlighten us?" One of the outlaw's barks back.

"I'm Saint James Street James, the deadliest motherfucker in all of the land. I had the highest bounty on my head in United States history."

"I know who you are! And I know what you look like! If you're really him, then why don't you show yourself?" Another outlaw quips.

"Fine. Look to your left in three, two, one!" I say as I jump out of the train.

When my boots hit the ground, I see all the outlaws turn and fire at Saint James Street Junior, blowing him to pieces. With their attention focused on him being shot so many times, I run around the corner and begin taking each and every one of them out with both of my pistols. After the smoke clears, not one of them is still breathing. I run over to Saint James Street James Junior who is coughing up blood and reach down to grab his hand.

"You did good kid. Just hang in there okay? I've actually seen a person survive something like this."

He looks at me and smiles. "Are you proud of me Dad?"

"Well, Ron would be. I'm kind of having a hard time with the fact that you weren't able to squeeze off a single shot right now. It almost makes me question whether or not you've ever actually discharged a weapon at all in your life."

He reaches into his pocket and pulls out a goat skin condom and holds it up. "I never got to use this," he says, barely able to breath.

"You should have never thought about using one in the first place. That was your first mistake," I whisper.

He nods his head and grabs a cloth from his pocket and places it in my hand, now unable to speak. His eyes roll into the back of his head as he takes his last breath. I gently lay his hand over his heart and open up the cloth. Embroidered on it is: **World's Best Dad.** To this day, I don't know if it was meant to be facetious or not, or if he genuinely meant it, but it gave me a huge laugh. Penelope races out of the train and runs up to us.

"Did you tell him to go that way on purpose because he looks exactly like you and you knew they would kill him?" She asks enraged.

"Of course not. Whenever I'm trying to give instructions for other people, it's kind of like a 'stage left' type of deal, which actually means the right, you know?"

"No, I don't," she says, genuinely pissed.

"Well, then I'm not going to apologize for your lack of culture within the arts. On a positive note, I just saved everyone's lives. Look at the whole train coming out to greet me," I say as I point to the smiling passengers starting to step off.

I raise a fist skyward, which draws a thunderous applause from within the train that comes flooding out the windows. The passengers begin to exit the train, cheering loudly. One by one they walk up and shake my hand as Penelope is pushed to the side. She shakes her head disgusted by my bravery.

"You want to start clearing those rocks while I sign autographs?" I ask over the adoring crowd.

She nods and begins begrudgingly clearing the rocks as I'm lifted onto the shoulders of the passengers. They carry me inside and begin to crack hidden beverages ranging from moonshine to whiskey. Our sleepy train car suddenly turns into an all out party. I get so goddamned hopped up that I decide to drive this fucking thing. With the conductor now dead, I figured why the shit not? DUI's didn't exist back then, so let's ride this fucking crazy train man.

When Penelope finally finished moving the last rock, I instructed the dude who took his shoes off to put Saint James Street James Junior in the last car, so I could box that son of a bitch up properly and send him back to Sheila. I'm sure she'll understand that he died for the good of the country. Now if *both* of his dads were dead and he lived, that would probably be even worse on him. At least that's what I wrote in the letter I placed inside the coffin later.

With a full on party now in full swing, we were off. I cranked up the train, ended up getting rail head* from a stranger, and then drove this bitch as far as it could take me—which ended up being the north eastern tip of Nevada. When the tracks ended, I was greeted by some cowboys who were waiting for our arrival. I pulled the brake and slowed us to a stop before zipping back up my pants and stepping outside. A gentleman in his 40's named Keith Coogan, nodded in disbelief.

"You Street James?" He asks from atop his horse.

"I am," I say, having trouble stuffing my cock back into my jeans.

"Name is Coogan. Keith Coogan. I work for Mr. Stanford. He said to keep an eye out for you," he says spitting tobacco juice on the ground.

"Well aren't you tougher than a four-dollar steak? How did you know I was coming?" I ask in a measured tone.

"Courier pigeon," he says pointing at his buddy next to him on a horse, politely holding a pigeon on a stick.

---

* Rail Head – Is a beej you get as a train conductor. It's an extremely rare and exclusive club. You're probably not a member of it like me.

"You tell that pigeon to keep his fucking mouth shut. If he starts passing notes behind my back about me, I'll blow him out of the fucking sky. You hear me?"

The two men look at each other, then at the pigeon. "Um, it doesn't really work like that. Anyway, we're happy you're here. No one has ever made it the length of the track yet. Goddamn robbers have derailed every train Mr. Stanford has sent."

"Not anymore. I'm here now, and we're going to build a fucking railroad," I say as I light up a smoke and hop on my steed, who has exited his train car on his own and strode over.

He laughs and and leans in to shake my hand. "If you can keep these deliveries up, it'll be a fucking miracle. Rumor has it that Jesse James has had his eye on these parts."

"Everybody has had an eye on these parts," I say as I motion toward my junk. "Fuck him."

"We'll take the supplies from here back to your men," he says as he tips his hat.

"Give them the day off once you arrive," I say.

Keith looks at me curiously, "Really?"

"Fuck no. Come on man. They're Asian, they can work forever!"

Both of us laugh simultaneously with deep, guttural, whooping cough-type laughter. His buddy actually hacks up one of his lungs onto the ground, which was hilarious and shocking at the same time. Know your audience.

If I said some shit like that today, I'd get a million genderless death threats and some bullshit speech from the head of the Laotian society at UC Berkley. But in the 1860's, casual racism was a nice ice breaker between strangers. You had a hearty chuckle and moved on with your fucking day.

As I said my goodbyes to Keith and finished my heater, I looked out over a weird camp town that was set up where the railroad ended. While my supplies were headed back to Samantha, another group of men were working here to extend the current track. This ragtag bunch of fuckholes were mostly comprised of Irishmen and ex-Confederate soldiers who could sense the war ending and headed west for work. Needless to say, these motherfuckers were wild. Penelope hopped on my steed and we headed into town for an overnight stay and some shuteye before heading out on the train back the following day. I already knew how this night was going to shake out.

When we checked into the hotel, one thing was abundantly clear; this shit heap definitely wasn't Omaha. Weird, right? That's probably the first time in your life that an individual has spoken aloud that they yearned for fucking Omaha, but it was true.

The hotel was actually split into two sections. Half of it was a whorehouse, the other half was for workers who were too poor to buy whores—or had already spent their money on them. The walls were as thin as Angelina Jolie after a hot yoga class, so you could hear everyone banging—or you could hear the dudes having a jerk sesh to the others *who were banging.* The noises that came out of there can only be described as a fat man jamming his fist into a full jar of mayonnaise at a rapid pace over and over. Let that image wash over you like holy water at a Southern Baptism.

I need a fucking drink worse than Ben Affleck, so I grab Penelope and venture downstairs to the hotel bar affectionately known as "**The Other Hole: The Good One That's Brown.**"

No lie. That was the name of the fucking bar. I knew shit was going to get rowdy when I walked in and an 82-year-old man was being thrown out the fucking window buck naked. A bunch of Irishmen cheered as he sailed through the glass out into the street. Penelope looked disgusted, but obviously I was used to this type of shit. I tap one of the Irishmen on the shoulder.

"What the fuck was that about?" I ask, pointing to the old man who is covered in blood outside.

"He kept saying all Irishmen are criminals. Fooking bastard," he said in a thick Irish brogue.

"But aren't they?" I ask.

"Yeah, but I stole his dentures earlier, so shouldn't have been able to say shit!" he laughs.

"Fair enough. I'd say he deserved it. Barkeep, round of shots for everyone!" The place erupts in cheers as I throw a stack of cash at the bartender.

The Irishman leans into me, "Say, where'd you get all that money? What do you own the whole fucking railroad or something?"

"Close enough. I work for the man that does," I say as I hold up a shot to the bar and chug it.

"Stanford? You work for fucking Stanford? Guess that means you'll be taking the train back then?" He asks.

"Yup, back and forth until this whole goddamn thing is built," I say pounding a shot.

"You ever take the train back before?" He asks.

"No. This is my first time heading out," I say.

He smiles and I can see a front tooth missing. After the bartender pours him his shot, he stands on top of the bar and raises his glass. "The man who bought us drinks works for Stanford, boys! He's never been on the train back!"

Another filthy Irishman in his late twenties smiles, also missing a tooth. "Never been on the train back you say?"

I don't know what the fuck is going on, so I answer more sternly. "No."

"Welcome to hell on wheels!" he says.

The bar erupts and some of men come up and pat me on the shoulder. They smell like the inside of a Jameson bottle. I went along with whatever the fuck was going on, figuring I'd find out later. Penelope seemed concerned, but she eventually got over it after a few glasses of champagne.

As with any good time, night quickly turned to day, and we never ended up leaving the bar until right before we were scheduled to head back west. We kick the doors open and head for the train somewhere in the 7am region. About thirty Irishmen and a handful of prostitutes come aboard the train back, which is always a recipe for disaster.

For some men, working on the railway was too big of a toll physically out there and they wanted to look for another line of work, while others headed back to see their families for a few weeks. Some of these dudes just wanted to settle down with the prosties they met in town and get married. They didn't want anyone else fucking them so they took them straight out of the whorehouse and got joined in unholy matrimony.

Within a few hours of the first whistle I understood why they called it "Hell On Wheels" back at the bar, people were getting fucked up all day and night. The amount of sex and flat out debauchery was of legendary proportion. I was going old school hard, punch a hole through a fucking wall type shit. The party from the bar didn't end until we hit Sacramento again. No fucking wonder no one ever robbed the trains back from these camp towns. They would have gotten their dicks beat in. Everyone was looking for a fight on these goddamn things. A bunch of people even ended up fighting each other just to do it.

When the train came to a stop back in California, everyone drunkenly spilled out and said their goodbyes, including Penelope. She couldn't really hang in that capacity with the booze and three-some's—sometimes four or five-some's—going on. I could tell she wasn't about that life.

"Can we talk Saint?" She asked politely.

Oh Christ. I know what that means. I'm bombed out of my mind, but I rub my eyes and pull it together enough to attempt a coherent convo. "Yeah, yeah, I'm good. Do you want a bump of gun powder or anything?"

She tries to laugh it off, but I can tell she wants to be serious. "No. I'm okay. Look, I think we should maybe say our goodbyes here, don't you think?"

"We're taking the train right back in an hour—

"I know, but I'm not really about that life. You said it yourself without quotation marks earlier," she says mocking me.

"Man, that was out loud again? Guess I got work on my inner monologue a little better," I say as I burp into my hand.

"And I have to work on getting reacquainted with a normal life again. This was fun, but it isn't for me. I need a one place where I call home and one man to do that with. I was fine with the soft swing thing the other night, but I don't want that to be a norm for me. I'll take Saint James Street James Junior back to Shelia for you," she says fighting back tears.

"Thanks for the offer. I'm sure delivering the body will come better from you anyway," I say.

"I don't know, it's her only son," she says softly, hoping for something else.

"Penelope, what if I said I was done with other girls and I want to give this a chance? A real goddamn chance," I say as I grab her hand.

She looks up at me in shock. "What? Are you serious? You said you didn't want to get married again?"

"What if I did, what would you say Penelope?"

Tears start streaming down her face, "Yes! I would say— *Wham!*

A fucking train smokes her coming from the other direction on the opposite track. She dies instantly and is then drug about seventy-five yards up the rails. Besides her hand, her boots are all that remain before me.

"Train!" an old guy in his seventies yells as he runs down hill out of breath.

"A little late on that heads up, wouldn't you say chief?" I say angrily.

"Sorry. They just installed a new loop here, but the damn thing is hard to stop. Oh well. Make it a great one today," he says as he waves a hanky at me before walking off.

At a loss for words, I sit down and stare at Penelope's hand. All I could think was, what if that was me? The other nugget that sifted through my grate was how nice it must have been to get a proposal right before you die. Honestly, I wasn't *really* proposing, I was just asking a hypothetical question—but to her it probably meant the world in that split second. Truth be told, I was pretty drunk *and in* Sacramento, and I just didn't want to be without company. This place is fucking boring.

Instead of taking Saint James Street James Junior back home to Sheila, I decided to put the casket in a nearby wagon and hitch it to my steed to take back. He's a fucking champ like that. Again, I'm super drunk, and I didn't want to really deal with that whole convo with Sheila after the morning I just had. My steed will catch the next train when I return.

Right now, I just need to get back on the train, have a fucking drink, and hopefully catch a few winks. It'd be rad if I could shake the image of my pseudo-girlfriend getting smoked by that train, but obviously I'm not counting on that for awhile, seeing how her hand is staring up at me like the *Hamburger*

Helper. The only thing I was counting, was how many days until this fucking Transcontinental Railroad is done so I could fulfill my promise to Lincoln... *and obviously become disgustingly rich.*

Chapter 14

THE GOLDEN SPIKE

April 4th^h, 1869

Promontory, Utah

After four fucking years of partying, killing hundreds of would be train robbers, and annihilating my liver night after night—this goddamn railroad was about a mile from being finished. I never want to ride a fucking train again after this shit. Nights turned into days, straights turned into gays—I'd seen it all and I was ready to be done with this shit. I just wanted one solitary place to lay my dong and call home. At this point, it didn't matter where. It looks like Penelope was right after all. I only wish she had the same foresight to see that train coming. Can't win them all I guess. The war has long been over now and I was ready to start somewhere fresh.

I squinted my eyes in almost disbelief as I stepped off the train from Sacramento to Utah. For the first time ever I could finally see the eastern track from my train coming west. It was almost done. One last fucking trip and this should all be over. Thank Christ.

As I begin to take a long celebratory piss into the dirt, in the distance I could see Keith Coogan riding up to greet me, as he had done every single trip before. Behind him was Samantha Davis and his crew, mixed with the Irishmen. I couldn't help but smile.

"You fucks coming to congratulate me? We're almost done with this bitch," I say as I extend my hand to shake his, still with my dick out. He shook it, because there was no washing your hands after pissing back then, so everybody had a little bit of dick on their hands.

"No, quite the opposite. We're here to warn you," Keith says somewhat forlorn as he shakes his head and looks at the ground.

"Warn me of what? Syphilis? I've had it three fucking times in the last four years, and for the last time, I'm not wearing a Jim hat. It just doesn't feel the same, and that's real talk—

"I'm not talking about sexually transmitted diseases Saint James, I'm talking about outlaws coming for you," he says remarkably worried.

"Who? I've killed every last one of them. Who else is left out there?"

"Jesse James and his gang," Keith says.

"Fuck you. I've heard this rumor for years and I ain't never seen him," I say as I pop a heater in my mouth.

"Apparently he's been biding his time. He figured the biggest ransom he could get was for that last mile of track seeing how the ceremony has already been set for next month. Folks really want to see this thing up and running. He knows Stanford would pay a good amount of money for that."

"Hell, I'd pay for it at this point. Look, I don't give a duck's shit about Jesse James or any of those pussies in his gang," I say as I zip up.

"The James-Younger gang is the most feared in all the west," he says in disbelief that I don't care more.

"Even that gang name sounds like shit. The 'James-Younger' gang? It sounds like Jesse got married and took his homosexual life partner's last name. If you're a goddamn man who's a fucking badass, it should just be your name—like me."

"All the same, you might be outmanned," Keith says.

Samantha steps forward. "I go with you boss. Me and my men are in," he says motioning to the Chinamen.

I nod at him like a father who pretends to be proud of their son hitting a single at a Little League game. "Look, you guys are great at hard labor, working painstaking long hours over and over again day in and day out, but you're not a street fighting men."

"Yeah, but we are!" a bunch of drunk Irishmen shout.

The response from the Irishmen actually peaks my interest. "Yeah? You boys ready to go against the feared James-Younger Gang," I say with absolute sarcasm.

"Fuck that guy and his lesbian partner," one of them screams out.

Laughter erupts from the group of men. "Life partners are hilarious and all, but would you be willing to die for what could potentially happen out there on these tracks?" I ask as I slowly walk past the men.

"Well it's not like we'd remember it anyway, so fuck'em!" another Irishman yells out. The Irishmen go even crazier now.

I take in all their enthusiasm and nod my head. "Alright then, who wants to mount up with the Street James Gang, because I'm not a fucking pussy who will hyphenate my last name?"

The camp goes ballistic. I unload my pistols in the air, inciting further unabashed admiration. Keith Coogan walks over and pulls me aside. I can tell by his demeanor that he isn't assured.

"Street, I've known you four years and I know what kind of man you are. You're stubborn, egotistical, and you think you can outgun anyone. Now in these last four years, you have, but Jesse James is a different individual," he says with a concerned look on his face.

"How is he different from me? I'm a man, dick and balls bigger than his—sight unseen—but that's a given. What makes you think he can beat me?"

"How much would you stand to lose off this last mile of track if this doesn't go through?" He asks.

"Two million," I say without flinching.

"Alright. And how much could Jesse possibly gain? A hundred thousand tops? What does he have to lose? Just send in another crew. It's not worth it," he says grabbing my shoulder.

Now I'm offended and I grab him by the collar of his shirt. "It's worth it to me. The last eight years of my life, the only man who gave me a chance to return to glory was President Abraham Lincoln. His last dream that he entrusted in me was to open up this railroad, and that's exactly what I'm going to do."

"And I understand that Saint James, but hear me out—

"We're all done here. The Irishmen will do just fine. I've been traveling with them for years now, and they truly do not give a fuck, same as me. I'd rather die trying at this point," I say removing his hand from my shoulder.

"Okay. I've said my peace. The decision lies with you; however, I cannot go with you. I got a wife and kids to think about," he says sincerely.

"Well, it's a good goddamn thing that I don't. That ground you're standing on is where my wife and kids are, and if Jesse James and his gang gets between me and my two million-dollar paycheck, he'll be right fucking there with them."

"Godspeed Street," he says as he tips his hat.

"Go on home to your family," I say as I walk over to Samantha and put my arm around him.

Samantha looks up and smiles. "Does this mean you want me and my men to come with you and help kill bad guys?"

"That's the most fem description I've ever heard about murdering dudes in my whole life. You have to work on not ending sentences in that high of a pitch," I say, shaking my head.

"Is that a yes?" He asks.

"Sure, but you're going to need these," I say as I pull out a handkerchief out of my pocket revealing three of his old teeth. They're the original wooden ones he made out of his father's boat.

His eyes well up with tears. "Where did you find them?" He says through his dirty lisp that I've always been annoyed by.

"Back in Coloma. You were probably crying so hard when you buried your burned up ancestors that they fell out. I found them amongst the ashes."

He rubs the wooden teeth made out of the deck of his father's old boat. "Thank you, Saint James."

I nod my head. "Your father would be proud of you right now. He wouldn't have been proud for almost everything you've done in the past, but he would be right now. Put the teeth in. I can't stand to listen to you speak with a fucking lisp anymore."

Without the slightest of hesitation, Samantha jams them into his mouth. He flexes his gums over the wooden teeth until he has enough saliva to speak, then he smiles at me like Tiger Woods to his caddy after a great fade. Sam's old confidence is back.

"Let's go fuck a butthole," he says as he fists bumps me.

I fist bump him back. "Indeed, Samantha. Let's put every single inch in." I point to the Irish and Chinamen behind him. "Boys, the drinks are on me back and forth from Sacramento!"

The Irishmen erupt in cheers like the crowd at a Dropkick Murphy's concert when the opening chords to *I'm Shipping Up To Boston* start. The Chinamen stood there motionless for a few seconds… *before immediately going back to work.* Nothing stopped those motherfuckers from working, not even free drinks.

Instead, I partied with the Irishmen solo at the bar. We got drunk, they fought each other, someone brought out bagpipes, then they killed him when he paused to take a breath. It was pure insanity.

The train ride back was even worse the next morning. I got so shit housed that I let one of them drive the fucking train home. He seemed legit at the time. I'll never forget his name, Shamus O'Malley. He was a living Irish stereotype. Red hair, always sunburned, you couldn't tell if he was thirty or sixty years old, and he is thick as fuck. After he knocked out the conductor, he cranked that bitch up to eleven and rode the damn rails as fast as a train could possibly go.

The Asians in the other car thought we were going to die. I could hear Samantha leading them in some sort of group prayer in Chinese. At least I think they were praying. They could have been coming up with new algorithms or ways to replace the abacus, who fucking knows. Either way, I didn't blame them. I was fully prepared to die on that train, so I'm not going to fucking judge. There was even one dude in the back of my train car who was jacking off as hard as he could while crying. I didn't fucking judge him either, that's how real this shit was. You really get to see someone's true colors during near death experiences.

When we finally made it back to Sac-town safely, Leland was waiting for me with five businessmen in suits at the train station. It was recently built to start accommodating actual paying passengers back and forth, since the railroad was soon to be open for business. These stations were now being built in a bunch of cities across America. The dream of the transcontinental railroad suddenly seemed very real.

As soon as I stepped foot on the platform, I was greeted with disdain for how drunk I was by Leland and his associates. This was the first time in four years that he had visited me in person on a back and forth trip. I fucking knew goddamn well why they were there too.

"Hello gentlemen. Surprised to see you here Leland. Those are nice suits. Who the fuck are these guys, the Brooks Brothers?" I say, trying not to slur my words.

"Actually they are. They're in town from New York for the ceremony, assuming that it will take place on time," he says visibly concerned.

"Why wouldn't it? I got one more track to deliver and we're done."

"Mr. Coogan told me that the James-Younger Gang was looking to stick it up and hold the last track for ransom," Leland bellows.

"That is strictly a rumor—

"Which causes us concern. How about I send back a Calvary to escort you?" He asks.

"How about you send back some escorts for my cavalry?" I counter, mocking him.

"I'm serious Saint James," he says through pursed lips.

"Not a fucking prayer. I've overseen this project for almost four years and I'll be goddamned if anyone escorts me downstairs like a velvet gloved lady trying not to step on her gown to finish the last mile, you understand me? I have my men, and they will be plenty enough for those assholes should they show up."

As I point to them, I turn and see four Irishmen pissing on each other, drunk out of their minds. Next to them are a handful of my Chinamen chopping the heads off of squirrels. Leland shakes his head.

"This is your crew? Jesus man. One of them is dead," he says concerned.

I look over and see one of the Irishmen lying face up on the platform, his face slightly pale and blue. "I made a promise to President Lincoln to see this through. If they do end up robbing the train, they're going to have to kill me to do it, and obviously because of my looks, they'll probably want to rape me after I die. So if I get killed and raped, by all means, send the cavalry. Until then, these crazy fucks are all I need."

Leland mutters something to the Brooks Brothers, and then shakes his head. "Alright Mr. Street James, but it would be a shame to see all your hard work go to waste. Four years is a long time trying to stay alive doing what you've done."

"Which is why I plan on being alive for the completion. One more thing, *when* I do complete the railroad, I want to drive the final spike into the ground," I demand.

He smiles at me, smug as fuck. "I'm scheduled to drive the final spike in, but sure, if you make it with this gang of misfits and drunkards, by all means the honor is all yours."

I extend my hand and he shakes it. Before heading off, I turn to the Brooks Brothers. "By the way, there's a bunch of dudes making better suits out of this men's warehouse in a camp town outside of Nebraska. You should give them a try. You're going to like the way you look, I guarantee it."

The Brooks Brothers scoff at me as I walk over to Samantha. "Sam, I need your help. I gotta go back to my old place to grab something."

He smiles and nods knowingly. "You need me to take a picture of you fucking Ron's wife?"

"What? No. Wait—do you have the ability to do that? I really don't have a nice portrait of myself sportfucking—actually, there's not enough time to get the lighting right and make it back in time. I need help with something else."

"Sure boss, what do you need?" He asks.

"Bring a hammer and chisel. I'll explain on the way."

Sam quickly gathers his tools and we head back to my place on my steed and another horse I took from the dead Irishman. It's not like he was using the goddamn thing again. We took the alt route home so I wouldn't have to pass Sheila's house.

Even though it had been four years now since Saint James Street James Junior had passed, and I'm sure she's probably over it, I didn't want to deal with that bullshit. She'd probably pull me inside for a sympathy screw, and of course I'd do it because I'm a fucking gentleman, then she would cry to me about losing her only son. Gross. Read a fucking book or something. I had more important things on my mind.

After the quick stop at my property, we headed back to the railroad where the Irishmen were raring to go. The bender they were riding was an all-timer at this point. These fucks didn't care about dying, and neither did the Chinese, who were now practicing rigorous karate moves in unison next to the tracks. It was like a scene from *Enter The Dragon*. Satisfied with exactly what the fuck was going on, I put two digits into my mouth and whistle loudly. Everyone stops and turns toward me.

"It's time for one more ride boys! Let's finish this fucking railroad. I'm emptying out the gun crates for anyone that needs them. All a-fucking-board!" I screamed out as loud as I could.

Samantha pops the crates on the emergency guns, which for the last four years, have gone unused. Every Irishman who came aboard took one, but the Asians declined. It was interesting to see the two different methods of battle preparation from each culture once they stepped foot on the train.

Once again separating themselves in two different cars, the Asians were calm and almost Zen-like. They took their seats, said nothing to each other, and remained eerily silent throughout the train ride back. The Irishmen on the other hand were the polar opposite, not only did they empty out the gun crate, they emptied out every last bottle of anything that even vaguely resembled liquor. They even set up a shooting range inside their fucking train car. It was loud as shit, but an effective tool for practice. This would be the last use of this supply train, so I just let it go down.

I sit in the back of the train car with the Irishmen and proceed to down a bottle of whiskey, mostly keeping to myself. It wasn't really my jam to sing fifteen different versions of *O' Danny Boy* over and fucking over. I know what you're saying to yourself, "Saint James Street James, *O'Danny Boy* wasn't even out yet at the time?" Relax your ball sacks, I know. Half the goddamn people in this train car were named "Danny", so it was only a matter of time before someone put pen to paper on that classic. I guarantee you the guy who wrote that fucking song was the only sober one in Ireland at the pub when someone busted that out for the umpteenth time. Good on you for jotting it down.

As the train chugs along through California and Nevada, I sip my whiskey quietly, thinking about the stories I had heard of Jesse James over the years. It was long known that he was a Confederate bushwhacker going from town to town robbing and executing Unionists after the war was over. He and his family had owned slaves, and those motherfuckers weren't content on doing work themselves after the war ended either. The typical nine to five grind didn't suit these backwoods assholes. They were going out in a blaze of glory.

It's not like I was afraid to face him or anything, but I had obviously heard the whispers over the years that he was the best, supplanting me from my rightful place at the top of the deadliest outlaw list. I understood the debate. He was twenty-one, I was cresting forty at the time. It was like Kobe guarding MJ at his first All-Star game, both of them wanting to prove they were the best. Any thought of death that crept into my mind was suddenly erased by the conductor screaming.

"Saint James, we got something on the tracks up ahead!" he called out.

The Irishmen fall silent as I make my way to the front of the train. I lean in next to the conductor inside his car to get a better look. He had his hand on the break ready to pull up. I squint my eyes trying to make out what it is. As the train inches closer, I am finally able to see it, and it was one of the biggest goddamn Clydesdale horses I had ever seen. It was lying there dead, stretched across the tracks.

"What do you want me do?" The Conductor asked.

"Drive through it. I don't want to take the risk that this could be a trap," I said as I pat him on the shoulder and walk back.

Before I could make it back to my seat in the Irishmen's train car, a gigantic explosion went off as we hit the horse. Someone had stuffed the fucking Clydesdale full of dynamite causing the entire train to derail. With the conductor car now blown to pieces, the passenger cars containing myself and the Irishmen tumble off to the right of the tracks, with the car containing the Chinese veering off to the left. Both cars land on our sides. As the first wave of Irishmen begin to make their way out of the top, gunfire erupts killing the first men out. We were fucking stuck in the middle of an ambush, and they just keep blasting away.

A few Irishmen smashed in front of me end up taking the brunt of the first rounds of bullets. I wait until the dudes outside have to reload to make my move toward a window at the top. My steed starts naying loudly outside as he begins sharply kicking the back of the train car letting me know he is there.

I draw both of my pistols and crawl out of the top, where I see about fifteen guys in the midst of their reload, so I begin blasting every shot I have toward them over my shoulder. Killing them immediately is an after thought, I was more focused on making it to my steed. Being stuck on top of the train car with no bullets does me no good. I need to be mobile. When I was out, I roll off the top of the train car backwards onto my steed.

Out of my peripheral, I can see the Asians helping each other out of their train car like acrobats out of *Cirque de Soliel*. Even in the heat of this intense battle I stop to notice their elegance and grace. Ten of them are able to climb out, including Sam, who is the last man out. They charge fast at the fifteen men like fucking ninjas. The first Asian flies toward one of the outlaws and round house kicks his horse in the face, sending him flying off.

The Asians were so quick and nimble that it caught the outlaws off guard. I'm not even going to front, I tripped out for a second when I saw that horse get kicked in the head. That was fucking rad and totally unexpected. One by one the Asians begin to attack the outlaws, taking them down from a top their horses. I quickly reload, dig my spurs into my steed, and tear out from behind the train car firing at two more outlaws, killing them dead as shit.

In the distance I can see Jesse James, who looks younger than expected, firing both of his pistols into the Asian wizardry that was taking place. This turned out to be the most brutal hand to hand combat I have ever witnessed. To my knowledge, martial arts had never really been introduced into the United States before now, but it was quickly getting introduced to the faces of these outlaws. It's hard to describe all the angles these guys were getting their fucking heads kicked in. Picture a John Woo film on acid.

From behind me, the remaining Irishmen slowly begin exiting the top of the train car. Jesse James pulls his gun on them and squeezes off a couple shots, killing the first two men out. I manage to return fire at him between the Asians and I'm able to hit his horse, bucking him off on to the grass. Since the others are engaged in hand to hand combat on the ground, I leap down from my steed and walk over to where Jesse has fallen, guns drawn.

He pops up as fast as he can, but I don't shoot him. A look of confusion crosses his face as I smile. I calmly holster both guns and stop about ten yards in front of him.

"What the fuck are you doing?" He asks as he raises his gun toward me.

"You Jesse James?" I ask.

"You know goddamn well I am!"

"Relax, you aren't that famous. Pro tip, you have to be good looking to be *really* famous. And you, well, you look like my entire nut sack if it were stretched out across a cutting board. If

I were blind, I could read your fucking pimpled face with my hands."

"I'm getting real sick of your mouth," he says angrily as he cocks back the hammer on his pistol.

"Which one is your homosexual life partner, Younger?" I ask as the Irishmen jump down from the top of the train car one by one.

A man who is beaten to a pulp slowly raises his head from underneath one of my Chinamen, who has just finished bashing his face in. "I'm Younger," he says spitting up blood. His nose is completely shattered.

"Sorry. It was hard to tell from underneath all that blood. Just out of curiosity, how did you decide whose name went first in the James-Younger gang, you go by cock size or who is a bottom first?"

"I'm going to fucking kill you!" Jesse yells.

All of the Irishmen cock their guns at once. I hold up my hand, motioning for them to hold their fire. "Let's find out if you can. Put your guns down boys," I say to the Irishmen. "I want to challenge this little fuck to a one on one, then we can really find out who the best is. What do you say?"

"I say you're going to end up with a bullet in your head friend," he says with a smirk.

"I'm not your friend and I'm not your power bottom fuck buddy like your dude on the ground over there. I'm the man who's going to take the last fourteen percent of your soul as soon as you say when."

"Fourteen percent?" He asks confused. "When—," he says as he draws his gun.

"Now," I say as I draw my pistol and fire it into his groin.

He hits the ground hard, unable to squeeze off another bullet. I walk over to him as he writhes in pain, holding his crotch. I stand over him looking down on him as if I'm about to empty my chamber. He's a helpless little bitch trying to conceal his tears. In this moment, the ruthless killer I've long heard about is gone, and all that remains is a scared kid hoping his mom will come and scoop him up.

I point my gun at his head, as the rest of the men look on. The Asians, Irishmen, and the few remaining living members of the James-Younger gang look on in disbelief. I cock back the hammer of my pistol and smile as he looks up at me, pleading.

"Just get it over with. Go on and kill me," he screams.

"Looks like I'm the only man that the rumors were true about. Pull down your fucking pants little man," I say as I motion with my pistol.

"What?" He asks as he looks up at me incredulously.

I holster my gun and kneel down next to him. "I'm not going to kill you. Pull down your pants and let me see where I shot you," I say.

"What the fuck is this?" He recoils.

"I can't kill a fellow outlaw. I'm not that fucking dude," I say as I uncock my pistol and holster it.

He nods understandingly. "Okay."

Jesse pulls down his pants revealing a bloody mess. The bullet is lodged into his thigh, and part of his scrotum and testicles are blown off. Fourteen percent to be exact. Damn it feels good to be a gangster. You know anyone else on the fucking planet who could call his shot like this? Fuck no you don't.

"Just know that I am the dude who took off fourteen percent of your testicles and let you know it before it happened. Every time you piss, jack off, or get your dick sucked—remember I am the man who took fourteen percent of your manhood away. Someday, someone else will take the rest. It just ain't going to be me. Now if you don't mind, I'll be taking those wagons you planned to use after you robbed us over there. I got a fucking railroad to finish."

I stand up and walk over to my steed. Jesse quickly pulls up his jeans and calls out to me, "Mister, I just gotta ask—why fourteen percent? What's the significance of that number?"

"That isn't your business. Let's just say that number is why I became an outlaw in the first place. Sam, take your men and load up the wagons. I'll tell Keith you're coming."

"Sure thing boss," Samantha says, still caught up in the moment.

I take off on my steed and you can be goddamn sure that I didn't look back once. Understanding your own legend is paramount in situations like this. I knew full well that every man out here today would tell every last friend, family member, and booze buddy this story for the rest of their lives. If I looked back in the slightest, it would have made me self aware of my own awe. Instead, I kept riding like the hardcore motherfucker that I am. My only regret is that there wasn't a photographer on site to capture my steed midstride with all this carnage in the background. Fuckin' A that would have made one hell of a mantle piece.

On May 10th, 1869 we completed the Transcontinental Railroad at Promontory Summit in Utah. I know, what a shitty town to complete one of the greatest feats in United States history. Chicago would have been bugfuck. New York would have rocked. Nope. Fucking Promontory, Utah. I stand there on the tracks and stare at the cheering crowd on the packed steps of the train station. Leland smiles and hops down, holding something wrapped in crushed red velvet.

He pulls back the velvet and smiles, revealing a large golden spike. "Congratulations. You've earned it."

"Thank you, but I actually brought my own," I say with a warm smile.

"What?" He asks confused.

I motion for Sam to come down off the platform. He nods and cuts through the crowd. You wouldn't recognize him now. I gave him some money and got him all suited up for the big day. He even has a sweet new set of temporary teeth.

Samantha walks over carrying something rolled up inside a piece of burlap. He hands it to me and bows. You can take the man out of China, but you can't take the China out of the man. I always appreciate a bow however. As I slowly untie the twine and unroll the burlap, Leland looks down in utter shock.

"Is that what I think it is?" He asks.

"Indeed it is," I say as I discard the burlap and pull a hammer out of the back of my pants.

"This is for you Totally Fucking Mexico!" I scream as I hold his fourteen carat gold arm up toward the sky.

The crowd erupts as I drive it into the ground completing the railroad. His arm was the perfect size and shape for the final spike. After I pound it in with my hammer, I fall to my knees. I can see his little body looking down on me from the sky.

"I love you father," he says.

"I know you do you son of a bitch," I say with a smile.

I throw up a fist in the air acknowledging his spirit and remove a flask of whiskey from my coat and take a long pull. Sam leans over and gives me a hug. He's clean, so I accept it and return said hug. This weird fucker has been with me since the get go, so the least I could do was return the admiration he probably felt towards me. After the release of our embrace, Leland lights up a cigar and hands me a check for two million dollars.

"Well Saint James, what are you going to do now that you're a very rich man?" He inquires with the kind of compassion that only another super rich man would have.

"I'm going to take this train to New York to try my hand at investing in the stock exchange," I say.

"Good luck. Don't get in over your head," he says wagging a finger a little too close to my face.

"Shut the fuck up *Leland*," I say with sincerity, before turning and boarding the train.

With Samantha right behind me, we sit down and remove our hats as other patrons start to board. This isn't the shitty supply train I was on back and forth to Sacramento, this thing was immaculate. You felt like you were in the lobby of a nice hotel, and for a brief moment, I caught myself impressed by what this actually meant for our country. I fucking did this shit, holmes. Unbelievable.

I take another deep pull from my flask and salute myself as I stare out the window in silence. I'm both mentally and physically exhausted from all this shit. The train ride back east will offer the first moment of true peace that I've had in a long time... *or so I thought.* A gorgeous woman in her early twenties walks onto the train car just as the locomotive roars to life. She sits in an empty seat across from me, smiling seductively.

"Excuse me, but aren't you Saint James Street James?" She asks.

"Since I delivered myself at birth," I say taking yet another pull of whiskey.

"Would you fancy a screw?"

"No, but I'll give you the whole goddamn spike. Sam, grab your camera and wooden tripod and meet us in the bathroom. I want to document this historical occasion. The first man to ever fuck on the Transcontinental Railroad. Now *this* is monumental shit."

She takes my hand and we head back toward the bathroom as the train takes off. Walking down the aisle I could see the excitement on the other passengers faces. Some of them were traveling east for the very first time, perhaps some seeing long lost family they've been unable to visit. Others were simply there for the excitement of a new found transportation across the country.

I was excited too. Excited to see what the future held. Excited that I survived this fuckery. Excited to be rich again. Above all else, I was excited to be banging out this dime piece in the bathroom. Let's face it, I deserve it.

Fin

EPILOGUE

Looks like you made through the book without retreating to a safe space. Good for you, fuckface. I know what you're thinking, "Saint James Street James, are you going to kill yourself now that this book is done?" Not yet, but I promise I will. There's a few more stories I want to tell about my life on this earth, but I can assure you, my death is imminent. I definitely won't be leaving this bar until I'm in a body bag. In my eyes, the world as we know it ended on a particular day long ago, and when I get to that date in my memoirs—I squeeze the trigger and end my existence. When you read what day it is, it will become painfully obvious to you. In your heart, you'll have known it all along. Until then, visualize me fucking that girl on the train until the next book drops. It was as glorious as you imagine.

CPSIA information can be obtained
at www.ICGtesting.com
Printed in the USA
LVHW09*2038190818
587435LV00004BB/34/P

9 780692 096666